A NEW PLACE, ANOTHER MURDER

A Sheridan Hendley Mystery

CHRISTA NARDI

ISBN-13: 978-1721836918
ISBN-10: 1721836918

Cover Design by Victorine Lieske

The Cold Creek Series by Christa Nardi:
Murder at Cold Creek College (Cold Creek #1)
Murder in the Arboretum (Cold Creek #2)
Murder at the Grill (Cold Creek #3)
Murder in the Theater (Cold Creek #4)
Murder and a Wedding (Cold Creek #5

Sheridan Hendley Mysteries by Christa Nardi:
A New Place, Another Murder (A Sheridan Hendley Mystery #1)

Stacie Maroni Mysteries by Christa Nardi:
Prestige, Privilege and Murder

The Hannah and Tamar Mysteries for Young Adults with Cassidy Salem:
The Mysterious Package (A Hannah and Tamar Mystery)
Mrs. Tedesco's Missing Cookbook (A Hannah and Tamar Mystery)
The Misplaced Dog (A Hannah and Tamar Mystery)
Malicious Mischief (A Hannah and Tamar Mystery)

CHAPTER 1

My complaints to my close friend, Kim, about boredom were interrupted by the slamming of the front door and I ended my call. Probably something I'd have to get used to as step-mom to a teenager. In the kitchen, I found Maddie, her backpack thrown on the floor. She was stomping around the counter island, her face in a pout.

"What's up Maddie?"

"You won't believe what happened today. It's unbelievable. I still can't believe it and I was there."

Her voice rose an octave as she vented and I had no clue what she was talking about. Maddie went to a variety of activities during the week. They were called "camps" but that seemed a misnomer to me. Robotics, theater, and computers were not quite what I thought of as a "camp." I waited a few seconds and she ranted some more.

"Alex was accused of stealing money from the office. It was in his backpack, but he didn't steal it. They didn't even give him a chance to explain. They called his mom and then took him away. He was mortified."

"Calm down and help me understand. Can we back up please? Who's Alex?"

"He's one of the kids attending all these camps with me. Of all the kids, he's been the nicest to me. I don't understand why they don't believe he had no idea how the money got in his backpack."

She finally simmered down and plopped into a chair, a grimace on her face.

"You may be upset for nothing. Once they got him to the station with his parents and got more information, they may have figured out they made a mistake. But why would they think he stole the money and why are you so sure he didn't do it?"

"I don't understand why they picked on him. The officer walked in and asked for him. Then asked where his backpack was. Alex pointed to his pack and the officer went over, opened it and pulled out an envelope and money fell out. It wasn't even hidden. Then they grabbed him. He looked around but nobody helped him. I didn't know what to do to help him."

"What makes you think he's innocent? How else would it get in his backpack?"

"You don't understand! Alex's nice. He … He wouldn't do that."

"How do you think the money ended up in his backpack then?"

"I'm not sure and Dad says I shouldn't accuse people without facts. When the police came and asked for Alex, two other boys snickered and fist-bumped. I think they set him up. All our backpacks stay in the main room while we go in and out. They could have stolen the money and stuck it in his pack. Then they must have called the police and made an anonymous report or something. We've got to help him."

She stomped around the kitchen some more and kicked her backpack.

"Maddie, is your backpack in the same place as Alex's and the others'?"

She turned to me and nodded. "Yeah, why? They're all together in the main room."

"Humor me, okay? Can you dump everything out of your backpack and make sure that the only things in there really belong to you?"

I cleaned off the table and she emptied her back pack onto the table. Books, brush, hair ties, crumpled up papers, pens, pencils, stale cookie, and an envelope.

"What? Where did that come from?" Her eyes opened wide. She went to grab the envelope and I caught her hand.

"Don't touch it. You don't know where the envelope came from or what's inside?"

She shook her head, eyes wide. "Am I going to get arrested now, too?"

"I don't think it will come to that. Your dad will be home in a little while and we'll show him what we found. He'll decide what to do. But don't touch the envelope in case there are fingerprints or something

CHRISTA NARDI

else that might help identify who handled that envelope, okay?"

She nodded and sat down, staring at the mess.

"Is that everything? What about the pockets? Everything out, even the crumbs." I realized this was going to be the cleanest this backpack had been since she got it almost a year ago. Maddie emptied and gasped as she found another envelope in one of the outside pockets.

"Sheridan, there's another one here. Oh, no, I touched the edge!"

"It's okay. Let me see if I can find something…" I rummaged through the kitchen drawer and pulled out serving tongs. "I'll use these tongs and pull it the rest of the way out." It took a few tries, but I managed to get the envelope out and dropped it with the other one. Then I released the tongs and left them on top.

"Now what?"

"Why don't you go through all the stuff you just dumped here and either throw it away or put it back in the backpack. Except the two envelopes. In the meantime, I'll work on finishing up the meatloaf and potatoes for dinner. Later, after we talk to your Dad, you might wipe the whole thing down with a sanitizer."

She made a face. "This cookie doesn't look so good. Did you make any more today?"

I looked at the cookie she'd picked up out of the pile. "That one bit the dust. Yes, there are more cookies over on the counter – only one, please. We'll be eating in an hour."

Somehow, my boring day seemed preferable to the drama. The idea of the camps was giving Maddie something to do. A big benefit, the camps provided an opportunity for her to make friends before starting at her new middle school in the fall. As with most 13-year-olds, middle school was a big deal. It was convenient she attended the camps at Clover Leaf Middle School where she'd be a student. And it had been working until then.

***

Maddie and I finished the dinner preparation and set the table as Brett pulled in the driveway. He raked his hand through his dark curly hair. That was a sure sign that he was tired or stressed. This situation with Maddie would push him over the edge, likely add a few gray hairs. Meeting him at the door, we kissed and that at least brought a smile to his eyes.

"Hungry?"

He looked past me to Maddie. I followed his gaze. Shoulders dropped and mouth quivering, she'd lost her independent teen, "I can take on the world" attitude.

"What's wrong?"

He'd barely got the words out and she was in his arms, sobbing. Her long brown hair fell over her shoulders.

"Maddie's friend, Alex, is in trouble. He's been accused of stealing money. Maddie thinks he's been arrested. The police found an envelope with money in his backpack."

"Do you want me to see if I can find out what happened with your friend?" He caught my expression and his jaw clenched. "That's not all, is it?"

"Afraid not. Maddie is sure he was set up, that somebody put the envelope in his backpack. When she told me both their backpacks were unattended in the room, I had her empty out hers. We found two envelopes that aren't hers."

His jaw clenched, he mumbled. "We'll figure this out. Let me call Chief Peabody and have him send someone over."

"I'll finish putting dinner on the table. I imagine they'll be tied up for a while."

Brett nodded and walked down the hall to our office. Maddie moved as if to follow him and I stopped her. "He'll take care of it and you can help me in the kitchen."

A few minutes later, he joined us. "There was a shooting. It'll be a while. Envelopes under the tongs?"

"We used the tongs so we wouldn't touch them."

He nodded. It was a quiet dinner, the envelopes grabbing our attention and dampening our usual dinnertime banter. We cleaned up and waited.

CHAPTER 2

It wasn't until about 9 o'clock when the Chief himself along with two officers showed up. Brett took the lead, having now heard the whole story from Maddie.

"Chief Peabody, good evening. I didn't expect you. Good evening, officers. This is my wife Sheridan and my daughter Maddie."

"Wish it were better circumstances. The situation became a little more complicated. But let's take a look at those envelopes to start with."

I pulled Maddie to me on the couch while the men moved into the kitchen. Something seemed off. They were a little more tense than I'd expected. I caught a word or two of the conversation and it sounded like the Chief was filling Brett in on the shooting. They came back in and joined us, Brett pulling up a chair in front of Maddie and me. The Chief and the officers stood on alert.

"Maddie, can you tell the Chief what you know

about Alex and the other boys you mentioned?"

"Alex is my friend. He lives in Westerfield with his mom and his sister, Karla. Of all the kids at the camps, so far he's been the nicest. He stood up for me when Luke or Caleb were bothering me."

Westerfield was another small community near by. Like Clover Leaf where we lived, it was not yet incorporated into Appomattox but enjoyed the benefits of the larger town.

Brett's face got red, but he managed to keep his voice low. "What do you mean bothering you?"

"They … they kept bothering me. Getting too close, playing with my hair… One time Alex saw what they were doing and he told them to give me space and leave me alone. After that, if either of them came near me, he'd manage to be at my side. We started hanging together."

"What else can you tell us about Luke and Caleb? And the envelopes? Tell us as much as you can remember."

"The police showed up and they talked to Mr. Simpson, and he got everyone's attention. He explained the police were here to search backpacks. Money had been stolen from the office and they'd gotten an anonymous tip it was someone in our group. I looked over to Luke and expected him to be nervous, but he smiled at me. We all waited. They asked specifically for Alex and his backpack. His was next to mine. They opened it, pulled an envelope out, and money fell on the floor. Then they took him away."

She got more and more upset as she talked. Hiccoughs started and we all waited for her to calm down.

"Anything else you can tell us?"

"Luke and Caleb – they fist-bumped and smiled as the police took Alex away. He didn't steal any money. No way did he do that. He's not like that."

"Sher, can you tell the Chief what happened when Maddie came home?"

I hadn't expected to have to explain anything. "Maddie told me what happened at school and suggested someone set Alex up. I asked her how that was possible. She explained all their backpacks are left in the room all day and nobody is in there when the kids go to different activities."

Brett nodded. "Go on."

I shrugged. "I asked her where her backpack had been the whole time and she said it was on the floor next to Alex's. I cleared off the kitchen table and told her to dump out her backpack. The first envelope was near the top as she dumped it out. I had her check all the pockets and there was another envelope. We used tongs to get it out. Neither of us touched the envelopes except maybe the edge."

Chief Peabody nodded and held up a bag. "These the envelopes and the tongs?"

I looked to Brett. "If those were on the table, yes."

Brett nodded and the chief confirmed.

"We'll check these out. Thanks for saving us some trouble." He nodded to his officers and Brett walked them to the door.

"Okay, it's getting late and we've had enough excitement for the day. Maddie, go take your shower and get ready for bed. We'll talk more then."

He gave her a hug. As she walked away, he tipped his head toward the kitchen and I followed him. Obviously, there was more to this story.

He sat down at the table, shoulders slumped, and his hands moved to his hair and stayed there.

"It's a good thing you found the envelopes, Sher. The shooting? It was of Mr. Lawrence Stories. They found a couple envelopes with money in them at the scene. Two boys were hanging around and commented the envelopes looked like the one police found in Alex's backpack."

At my raised brows and stare, Brett added, "Luke Buchanan and Caleb Buchanan – they're cousins. They also said someone suggested Maddie was involved. By then though, I'd already called about the envelopes."

"So now Alex is not only accused of theft but murder? And they implicated Maddie?" I could tell my voice was rising and Brett signaled with his hand for me to bring it down.

"Yup. And they found a gun in the dumpster outside Alex's house after another of those anonymous tips."

"Oh my gosh! Is it the gun used to kill Stories? What would his motive be?"

"Possibly the same gun. Ballistics won't be back for a while. The Chief said it looked to be wiped clean. They'll be checking for any traces though. Motive? I'm not sure. Unfortunately, Maddie is now implicated as well. What do you think? Should she go to camp tomorrow? If so, I think it's time I showed up at this camp and introduced myself."

Maddie joined us as he finished. "No, Daddy. You can't come in and tell everyone you're a detective with the State Police! No one will ever be friends with me. Why shouldn't I go to camp tomorrow? Did you find out what happened with Alex?"

Brett took a deep breath. "This is a lot more complicated now, Maddie. The shooting I mentioned earlier? It was a man and he had envelopes like you and Alex had. Luke and Caleb showed up at the scene. They'll give their statements tomorrow with their parents present, but they mentioned you and Alex. I think it would be best if you stayed home for a day or two. The police need to sort out the whole money thing."

"Oh no. I didn't like Luke. He was friendly, but he wasn't nice and Caleb is just creepy. They don't think Alex killed the man, do they?"

"No idea, Maddie. You okay keeping Sher company tomorrow and Friday? Hopefully, this will all be sorted out by then."

Maddie wasn't all smiles, her mouth in a pout at the idea of hanging around the house all day.

"Wait a minute. I talked to Kim just before Maddie got home. She suggested I come visit. How about coming with me for a visit to Cold Creek? Maybe have lunch with Kim and Marty?" I'd worked

11

with Kim Pennzel at Cold Creek College until Brett and I married and I moved to his house in Clover Leaf. Maddie knew Kim and her friend, Marty.

That brought a smile to her face. "Okay, that might be fun. Before we go though, it's too late now, but I'll need to call Alex and make sure he's okay."

Brett's mouth dropped. "You can try in the morning before we leave. He may be busy though."

"Well, if he goes to camp and I'm not there, I'm sure he'll call me." She nodded her head as she talked. "I'm tired. Good night." She went to her room and we heard the door close.

"I still think I need to go in and scare some of these kids."

"You could do that this time. Maddie may be right though. It could make her a social pariah if you go in all gang-busters."

Brett didn't respond, so I added, "It might stop the boys in this class or the next class. What about all the times in the future when Maddie may need to stand up for herself or defend herself?"

CHAPTER 3

Kim was good for lunch and I looked forward to seeing her and Marty. With a subdued Maddie, the hour trip to Cold Creek dragged. I tried to liven things up by turning on the radio, only just my luck, there was a news alert about the murder. The alert stated there was a suspect in custody. Then the station cut back to music.

"Do you think they mean Alex? How could they?"

"I know, Maddie. It's hard when a friend is accused of something bad. What can you tell me about Alex, other than he stood up to those bullies."

"He's nice. Same age as me. He doesn't talk much about his family, but he has a sister, Karla. She's in fifth grade. They got fellowships to attend the camps this summer. His mom is a nurse and works lots of hours. A neighbor lady watches them sometimes."

"What about his dad?"

Maddie hesitated before she answered. "His dad left and hasn't returned. I think Alex said that happened when he was in third grade. I got the feeling maybe he was in jail from some comments Luke and Caleb made."

I cringed, but shifted the conversation. "Okay, well tell me about Luke and Caleb."

"I don't get them. Luke is like real cute and popular. He acted friendly. At least that was what I thought the first week. The other girls, especially MaryJane, were all over him, inviting him to join us for lunch. He was in a different group the first week so I only saw him at the beginning of the day, lunch, and at the end of the day. He seemed okay then."

"It sounds like you changed your mind. What happened?"

She didn't answer right away and I waited. She took a deep breath. "I heard MaryJane stop Emma from following Luke outside. It wasn't what she said, but her tone – it kind of scared me."

She stared out the window for a few seconds and then she continued. "He always seemed friendly though, talking with everybody, and he started talking to me. I think he goes to Clover Hill Academy. He and Caleb both. They'll be in 10th or 11th grade, I think."

"Oh, so he and Caleb are older than the rest of you? Why would they be at the same camps as you and not doing something else?" I wasn't familiar with Clover Hill Academy other than it was a pricey private school.

"Luke called the camps 'glorified babysitters' once. He made a comment about how they were being punished by having to come to the camps. Rich, I think. Luke also made a comment about how Alex was from the poor side of town."

"Maddie, you still haven't told me what happened between you and Luke."

"It was nothing. Really. Nothing. Mostly like I said, too close sometimes. Then one time, I forgot something in the computer lab and ran back to get it. Luke followed me. I turned around and collided with him. He made me uncomfortable. He didn't back up and held my arms so I couldn't back up. Alex came in." She shuddered.

"Alex walked over and asked what was going on. Luke hissed at him to go away. Alex told him he wasn't leaving without me. That must have surprised Luke. His grip on me loosened and I bolted. Alex had a cut lip when he came back, but he never said how it happened. After that, Alex pretty much never left my side. Word spread around among the girls not to leave alone or go anywhere alone with Luke."

Now it was my turn to shudder. "Did you or anyone else report his behavior?"

"Geesh! Nothing. Really. Happened. I'm not going to 'report' he looked at me funny and made me uncomfortable. If he did something and someone reported it, I didn't hear about it."

"I'm glad Alex was there to help you out." Maddie sang along with Justin Beiber and I took the hint. We were almost to Cold Creek and I'd ask about Caleb on the way home.

"I know we're visiting my friends here, but was there any place you wanted to see or anything you wanted to do?"

"Can we drive by your old house and see if the new people did anything to it? You know, like painted it a weird color?"

I laughed. "Sure, we can. Maybe it's purple or pink now with flamingo statues on the front lawn."

She giggled. I drove down the street and slowed as we approached what had been my house. Nothing had changed except for the red SUV and the pink tricycle in the driveway.

***

At the Grill, our most popular place to meet up and eat in Cold Creek, Zoe greeted us with hugs.

"We've missed you. Please, please take a seat with your friends. I'll get you coffee. And Maddie, I'll get you lemonade. Just like old times."

Zoe was all smiles as were Kim and Marty. Kim's red hair and high energy, combined with Marty's dark hair and more serious approach to life made them a poster couple for opposites attract. More hugs and food ordered, Kim filled us in with updates on the happenings at the college.

"Things are pretty quiet since you moved. Have you heard? Jim is finally going to retire. Nobody's quite sure if that was his choice or if it came down from above." Kim shrugged.

"So, who will take his place? You?"

"All that administrative stuff you did year round is not fun."

I chuckled. When I left Cold Creek College, Kim inherited my office and the role of unofficial assistant department head for the Psychology Department.

"You should have figured that out watching me."

"I think you hid some of it very well. The meetings alone are making me crazy. No way do I want Jim's job." She paused and her mouth twitched. "Hold on to your seat. Can you imagine Max as department head?"

"What? I thought he was determined to leave?"

Also a faculty member at Cold Creek College, Max tended to overreact to anything that was out of the ordinary. He even looked the part, with his dark hair always in need of a cut and often quite wild. To say the least, he kept things lively at the college. Although he tended to be obnoxious, he'd shown he had a good heart on many occasions.

"Guess he figured if he couldn't leave, he'd move up to administration? But enough about Max. How are you doing, Maddie?"

"Okay. Appomattox is okay." She looked over at me with a smile. "It's great to have Sheridan there." The past spring had been filled with changes for Maddie. First, her mother had decided Maddie should live full-time with Brett and then with our marriage, I moved in with them along with Charlie, my sheltie.

"So where exactly do you live now? What's the history?" Kim rolled her eyes at Marty's question and I obliged, honing in on one of Marty's history interests.

"In Appomattox County. One of the popular historical sites in Appomattox is the Appomattox Court House National Historical Park, the site of Lee's surrender to Grant toward the end of the Civil War. The Historical Park is also referred to as Clover Hill, the original name of the town. One of the oldest historical markers is at the Clover Hill Tavern – it dates back to the 1800s. We live in Clover Leaf nearby so it isn't far to get to the historical park or any place else."

"The local dog rescue is right there, too." Maddie added and with a quick look down excused herself.

"Everything okay, Sheridan? She seems kind of off today – not the usual bubbly Maddie. And she just bolted."

"I saw her glance at her phone. There have been some problems at the camp she's been going to and then a friend of hers was arrested for stealing money. It seems to have been a frame to get him in trouble. Then, well remember how Max keeps saying I'm a magnet for murder? Well, he may be right."

"What do you mean? You found another body?"

"No, I didn't find a body. Someone was killed last night. Two other boys from camp mentioned Maddie and her friend to the police at the scene. She hasn't heard from her friend since he was arrested yesterday."

Kim glanced toward the restrooms. "She seems to be taking a while. You worried?"

"I would be but she took her phone with her. I'll

give her a few minutes. She's upset about Alex and may be trying to call him to find out what's happening."

"Alex? That's her friend?" I nodded and Kim asked, "What's your plan?"

"I don't have a plan. I'm not getting involved if I can help it. I'm not familiar with the juvenile system in Virginia. I'm pretty sure it doesn't work exactly the same as in Delaware." Before working at Cold Creek College, I'd worked as a psychologist at a residential facility in Delaware and many of the youth there had been involved in the juvenile system.

Marty cleared his throat. "I'll see who I know in the juvenile area and get you the information if I come up with anything. Maybe at least an attorney for him if he ends up needing one."

I hoped Marty's contacts would come through. Only in Clover Leaf for a month or so, I hadn't met very many people yet.

"What are you up to? Kim mentioned you seemed kind of down yesterday."

I glared at Kim for sharing that. "Mostly? I've unpacked. Needless to say, I took over the closet in the master bedroom and rearranged the room a bit. Brett's still getting used to the idea clothes now hid his small gun safe in the closet. And, before you ask, yes, he's still trying to get me to learn to shoot."

"Any job prospects?"

"I've put in applications at the local colleges and community colleges. So far nothing is open. I'm hoping something comes up by the end of the summer. It's a waiting game for now. Patience is not one of my virtues, and I am already bored."

"Have you considered other things to keep you busy in the meantime?"

"Volunteer work in the community. Other than the animal shelter there doesn't seem to be a lot of easy opportunities. You know I'm a sucker for dogs. So far, my main activities are playing with Charlie and volunteering two days a week at Clover Hill Pets and Paws. That doesn't take a lot of time."

The conversation ended as Maddie returned, not happy or talkative. As we finished eating in silence, I noticed Marty nudge Kim. She smiled, reached below the table, and pulled out a photobook of Brett and my wedding. Maddie had been our wedding planner and she beamed as we looked through the pictures.

Lunch over, we hugged all around with assurances we'd be in touch. I definitely wanted to hear more about Max as possible Department Head. His tendency to hysteria would not make for a positive work climate. Zoe had a to-go cup of coffee for me and lemonade for Maddie. Good thing it was only about an hour ride to get home.

CHAPTER 4

The clouds had come in while we ate and weather alerts for thunderstorms started coming in as we left Cold Creek. With a glance to Maddie, I said, "Well …?"

"I tried to call Alex. His sister, Karla, answered his phone. Sheridan, he's back in detention and Karla thinks they want to put him in jail as an adult. We have to help him. You've helped others before. I'll help you."

"Did she have any news about the money?"

"She only said he was released and came home. Then the police came back last night and arrested him again. Mrs. Champlin took the day off from work and Karla didn't go to camp today. What are they going to do? They can't afford an attorney. What will happen to Alex?" Her voice got louder as she spoke and finally broke with her last question.

"Maddie, maybe the police have learned

something more today. Your dad is looking into it, I'm sure. They will find other people with a motive. This takes time. Remember how long it took for the police to figure out who killed the director of the community theater?"

"Yes, but you helped prove Isaac was innocent and identify the killer. Will you help Alex? At least talk to him?"

"We'll see what your dad found out and how he feels about it, okay? And what happened with the money in your backpack. Making sure you aren't involved or in danger will be the priority."

"Okay, but I feel so helpless and like it's my fault some how. I have to do something to help him."

"All you can do is support him and Karla. In the meantime, tell me about Caleb."

She exhaled and her mouth set. "Luke and Caleb hung together. I… Caleb isn't as cute or charming. He's big and clumsy and scowls a lot and he gets too close sometimes. He smells funny, too."

"Has he ever touched you, Maddie?"

"Nope. Never. It's creepy. Like he's within inches and hovers there, ready to pounce. Then he doesn't. I can smell him – something sweet. And he does it with all the girls, not only me. We all move and then he moves. He doesn't say anything. He's just there, usually behind us. Creepy like I said. I've turned around and said 'hi' or something to him. He responds with 'hi' back or answers a question if I ask one. Then he stands there."

"How did he and Luke get along? Did they kid

around with each other? High five or fist bump all the time?"

"Mostly they seemed to be whispering to each other. Honestly, it may have been nothing, but when they were apart from the rest of us and all secretive, I figured they were cooking up some kind of scheme." She shrugged her shoulders. I suspected she was right.

"Did they ever fight or argue?"

"With each other? No, not really. When Luke would be charming the girls, Caleb would scowl. Mostly they argued with the teachers. All the teachers. Over the rules, over the time an activity started or ended, over the food they served, over anything. That was their version of fun."

"What did everyone else do when they argued – the two of them confronting the staff?"

"Except for the food stuff, most of us weren't impressed and ignored it. Sometimes the food was pretty bad or cold when it should have been hot. Then some of the others chimed in."

She turned on the radio and started singing. Conversation ended and my thoughts reeled. How were Luke and Caleb involved in the murder? Did they murder Stories and then decide to frame it on Alex? That seemed too simple.

***

Brett picked up take out for dinner so we could avoid going out in the storm. One of Maddie's favorites, he'd gone to Seafood Grill and Deli and brought home seafood pasta salad, grilled shrimp, and coleslaw. He asked about our trip and we showed him

23

the photobook. He was as surprised as we were and the three of us paged through and talked about all the people in the pictures.

Brett asked Maddie to create a thank you note for all of us to sign. She was more than happy to comply and disappeared, Charlie following behind. With Maddie occupied in the office, he helped me clean up and put away food.

"I got a call from Chief Peabody today. The money found in Maddie's bag?" He looked toward the door to make sure she wasn't there before he continued. "There was residue of cocaine on the bills and inside the envelopes. At least that's what they think. The lab will have to officially document it. The officers who arrested Alex hadn't paid attention, only counted the money. Once they saw the residue on the bills Maddie had, they checked the other batch. More residue. Looks like whoever planted the envelopes might be into drugs."

"But I thought the money was stolen from the office?"

"That's another story. The receptionist reported $200 stolen from the office to pay for the pizzas delivered all month. Pizza Heaven let her charge the pizzas and she was going to pay for them yesterday. When the money was gone from her drawer, she called the police to report the theft after alerting Mr. Simpson." He paused before he continued for effect.

"The police showed up minutes later, after receiving an anonymous tip. Timing was a little too quick since Mr. Simpson hadn't said anything to the students yet. And there was $250 in the envelope in Alex's backpack."

"Huh. So, the money was planted – that's the assumption at least – before they actually stole the money so they didn't have any idea how much to put in the envelope? And obviously, they planted even more with the two envelopes in Maddie's backpack. Any prints?"

"None of the prints were very good. They only got a partial, so any match would be inconclusive. There was another $400 in Maddie's envelopes. Chief Peabody talked to the responding officer. He'd been told $200 was missing and the tipster pointed to both Alex and Maddie. When he found the money in Alex's pack, he stopped looking. He was pretty sure he had it all and never considered he'd found more than was stolen."

I felt my mouth drop. "So, they were setting both of them up with a single tip? And Chief Peabody believes they stole the money even though they found more money than was stolen?"

"No. That's the thing. Now they think somehow Alex thought it was Stories who set him up, albeit with help from Luke or Caleb. And the money was all related to drug deals given the possible cocaine traces. Obviously, there's no way to determine if the $200 from the office is even in there. The police are saying it was coincidence."

"What?" I knew I was getting louder again, but this was ridiculous. Chief Peabody hadn't seemed as much a nitwit as Chief Pfeiffe in Cold Creek.

Brett was about to respond and Maddie returned with the thank you note she'd designed. She wanted us to pick one picture from the wedding to put on the thank you.

I found one of Kim, Maddie, Brett, and me. She ran off, with a "Be right back." This time Charlie didn't follow but went to the door and I let her out.

"Where does that leave Maddie?"

"Oh, they suggested Alex befriended her so he'd be able to stash part of his money in her pack."

I opened my mouth and Brett put his hand up.

"Lots of questions and, so far, the whole case against Alex is circumstantial. The kid wasn't released from detention until almost 5 and the shooting took place around 6. His mom says he was home then. They don't know if she's telling the truth or protecting her son. They're talking to the receptionist again and then neighbors."

CHAPTER 5

Focused on my laptop screen, I jumped when Brett's hand touched my neck. "What's up?"

"You startled me. I'm trying to figure out the Virginia juvenile justice system. Website is not overly helpful."

"The bottom line? He was released pending arraignment for theft and then detained again. There'll be a detention hearing on Monday. Rule is three days, but nothing happens on the weekend, so he's stuck there." He rubbed his jaw.

"I can tell from the look on your face, there's something else."

"With two charges against him and one of those murder, the hearing will be used to determine if he should be tried as an adult."

I gasped. "He's 13 years old. What factors go into the decision?"

"The one working against him is the seriousness

of the crime – the homicide. No idea if he has any previous history in the system. That would be another strike. Two arrests in the same day, another strike. On the other hand, his age works for him."

"But, Brett, all the evidence is circumstantial. Two anonymous tips? Where'd he get the gun and in such a short amount of time? What did he have to do with Stories?"

"I know, I know."

"Maddie asked me to help him." I left it out there and waited.

Brett exhaled. "First, we need to make sure she is in the clear and safe. Can we agree?"

I smiled. "I already told her that was the first priority."

***

While I waited for Maddie to wake up of her own accord, I cooked some bacon and scrambled eggs. We were about to sit down to eat, when Maddie stumbled into the kitchen. I pushed the plate in her direction, grabbed some orange juice for her, and scrambled more eggs. Her long hair was in tangles and she had bags under her eyes. My feeble attempts at conversation were met with grunts.

When she finished, she put her plate in the sink. "I'm not going to camp again, am I?"

"Not the best idea. Today is my day to help out at Clover Hill Pets and Paws. I thought you might come along." I petted Charlie while she thought it over.

"Okay. Does Charlie get to go, too?"

"Afraid not. The dogs at the shelter don't get a lot

28

of human attention and affection. It wouldn't be fair to them or Charlie to bring her and then not give the others the attention they need or neglect Charlie. We can take Charlie for a walk later though."

She nodded in response and looked around.

"Go ahead and get dressed. I'll clean up in here and feed Charlie." She hesitated and then disappeared. I took care of the kitchen.

In no time, we were on our way, Charlie reluctantly left at home. Although the sun was bright, there was a nice breeze and it wasn't too hot. We arrived at the older building that housed Clover Hill Pets and Paws. Originally a colonial home, the downstairs now had concrete floors, sealed and stained in slate blue. The entry way included a small reception like you might see at a hotel. Mrs. Chantilly greeted us.

"Well, look at you both. How are you Sheridan? This must be Maddie. Welcome to Pets and Paws. Our residents will be happy to see you." Mrs. Chantilly reminded me of what Mrs. Claus would be like. An older, grandmother type, she was all softness and light. Except when someone brought in an injured animal. Then she was all business. I'd only seen that once in the month I'd been volunteering.

"Yes, Mrs. Chantilly, this is Maddie. She's going to help out today. Where shall we start?"

She smiled and her face lit up. "I'll see if Susie can give Maddie a quick tour, show her where everything is. Then she can help with the three mamas and their pups in the side room. Those pups love to play."

She paused. "As for you, grab yourself a coffee and you can work the bigger dogs in the back. Not as cute, but just as much in need of attention. Melina is back there."

I looked over at Maddie and she nodded. Mrs. Chantilly was already on the phone to Susie, a college student. I knew Maddie would be in good hands and watching puppies was sure to put a smile on her face.

Leaving Maddie with Mrs. Chantilly, I made my way into the kitchen. A bit more modern than when the house was first built, it was functional rather than fancy. Cabinets had been renovated to be more like lockers and I shoved my bag and keys in one of them.

I could hear the deep barking of the larger dogs as I walked down the hall to what I guessed was originally a living room or great room. Instead of stately furniture, it now had large dog crates. I set my coffee and phone down as Melina came in the back door with Razor, a beautiful black Newfoundland.

About my age I guessed, Melina was down to earth, with shorter dark brown wavy hair and brown eyes. Like me she wore shorts and a t-shirt to work with the dogs.

"Hi, Sheridan. Great to see you! Razor here is all set. Cage cleaned out, he's had some playtime, and I even managed to get him a bath. The rest of these guys…" She guided Razor back into his space with ease, despite her slim and petite frame. Razor looked to outweigh her, but obviously was a gentle boy.

A quick look around and it was obvious Chloe needed some attention. "I'll start with Chloe. It doesn't look like her run has been cleaned out in a while." A mix of Brittany and something, Chloe's coloring resembled a brown and white cow. Now spayed, she'd obviously had pups along the way. I reached for her door and she sat quietly, her tail wagging. I got her outside into another run and Melina got Buster, breed unknown outside as well.

As we each cleaned out the dogs' runs, Melina commented, "Awful what happened in the historical park, isn't it? That man murdered."

"Sure is. What have you heard about it? You're from around here. Did you know him or his family?"

"Mr. Stories was married to one of the Buchanan girls." She nodded like that said it all.

"Melina, I'm new around here. Who are the Buchanans?"

"Well now, the Buchanans are one of the older families around here. Some historian traced them all the way back to the War, the confederate side, I think. They didn't suffer any financial hardship though." She paused to take a breath.

"The Buchanans own the Sleep Softly Inn, as well as two of the other hotels in town, the Steakhouse over in Sleepy Hollow, and pretty much all the real estate business in Appomattox County. Blake Buchanan was Mayor of the town when I first moved here. Probably half the town council members are related to the Buchanan family somehow."

"So where does Mr. Stories fit in?"

"Oh, Blake Buchanan had three sons and one daughter. He talked on and on about the boys, especially Brandon and Delaney, not as much about Shane, and never about Lila. If you couldn't play football, you weren't important. She was schooled in all the proper manners and such though. She went to college. I think she's still involved in the arts." Melina turned to check on the dogs.

"Anyway, she graduated from UVA and got a degree in something. That's where she met Lawrence Stories. They were married the next summer, first son born a year later. I'm not sure, but I think there are three Stories boys, one of them graduated last year and enlisted in the Navy. Blake Buchanan wasn't too happy. Wants all his children and grandchildren to go to college and be professionals."

"Is one of them named Luke or Caleb?"

"Luke is the son of the Blake's oldest, Brandon. Caleb is a cousin, son of Delaney – Del – Buchanan, I think. All the sons had sons. Seems to run in the family, except for Lila and I think one other girl, a cousin to Lila."

"The Buchanans sound powerful. Do you think someone killed Mr. Stories to get back at the family somehow?"

"Hard to say. I only know what I hear and read in the paper or on the Internet. Didn't ever have anything to do with them personally. They pretty much stick to their own. Started the private school on the edge of town so they wouldn't have to mingle with the rest of us." Her usual smile morphed into a frown.

"Melina, how old are your children? Isn't one of

them in middle school?"

She smiled and her whole face lit up. "That would be Nedra. She is a great student. Starting 8th grade in the fall at Clover Leaf Middle. Hard to believe how fast they grow up." Still smiling, she shook her head ever so slightly.

"Maddie will be entering 8th grade at Clover Leaf, too. How is Nedra dealing with the murder?"

"We don't talk about it much. When we first heard, Willie commented it was a sad thing for someone to be killed. Nedra made some retort about Luke Buchanan but then wouldn't explain it. May have been some bad blood there."

As she finished, Mrs. Chantilly joined us with a tray of homemade dog treats. "You talking about the murder over in the park?"

We nodded as we both picked up dog treats and gave them to the dogs, saving two for Chloe and Buster.

"Those Buchanan boys are spoiled, especially Shane. No sense of responsibility and I have to wonder at the treatment of their horses." I'd noticed Mrs. Chantilly had a tendency to jump from one topic to another. Sometimes her line of thought was hard to follow.

"Horses?"

"Oh, not here in town. But some of the Buchanans are into the horse racing circuit, breeding and such. The Buchanan men have not always had a good reputation in their treatment of women. Big scandal a few years back. But I'll let you ladies get back to our charges here. I don't know much about the Stories fellow though."

We both nodded as she floated away with her tray to the next room in the house and other dogs. Finished with Chloe's cage, I stacked a clean blanket and dog bed by the gate and headed outside to play some catch. Melina joined me and we chatted about Nedra and Maddie and the inevitable challenges of raising teenaged girls as we played with Buster and Chloe.

CHAPTER 6

By the time Melina and I finished up with some more of the big dogs, my coffee cup was empty and I was in need of a recharge. Coffee and then checking on Maddie were my priorities as I entered the kitchen.

Maddie was there and all excited. "Oh, Sheridan, the puppies are so cute. They try to climb into my lap and fall over. Susie says they haven't gotten their balance yet. So warm and cute. One mama is doing well but there are eight pups. One of the pups doesn't seem to get to feed a lot. I got to bottle feed him so he can get bigger. Can we take him home when he's big enough?"

"I'm not sure about that, Maddie. We'll have to talk to your dad. Taking care of a dog is a big responsibility and I'm not sure Charlie would like having a puppy around."

"But you'll talk to dad, right? And we can bring Charlie here and see what she thinks? Two of the other puppies are already spoken for and Susie doesn't think the littlest one will get adopted." Her mouth turned down and her eyes big, Brett was in for trouble.

"We'll see what happens. Was there only one mama with pups? How about we keep working for another hour or so and then we can get some lunch?"

"Okay. There are two other mamas, but the other pups are older. I was helping with the little one."

I nodded and she ran back to the mama and her pups. I was sipping on my coffee when Mrs. Chantilly came in.

"Terrible thing about the murder. My daughter, Lacie, she works at the police station and she told me they arrested Alex Champlin. The family has had enough problems and Alex wouldn't hurt a flea."

"Maddie knows Alex from the camps she's been going to and she said the same thing." I waited and hoped she'd say more.

"He's polite and respectful and smart. His mama, she works hard and he helps out around the house, mows lawns, and takes good care of his sister, Karla. Those Buchanan boys could learn something from him."

She shook her head. "The daddy, Kobe Champlin? He got himself in all kinds of trouble. Drugs and stuff. He went to prison and died a couple years ago. No help to his family. And Angie, she's stayed strong for those two kids. Lacie told me the local pastor was already in to see Alex and to have a talk with Chief Peabody."

Melina walked in as Mrs. Chantilly finished up. "Chief Peabody is taking his time to make sure he has all the information. He may be thorough, but he's not stupid. He'll figure this out with or without help from those Buchanans."

"Maddie mentioned Luke Buchanan, said he was real friendly."

The two women exchanged glances and Melina nodded to Mrs. Chantilly to respond. "Maddie's gonna turn a lot of heads and get attention from a lot of these young boys. Luke knows he's good looking and he's a charmer – underneath the charm, he's a snake. He has a reputation for taking advantage and he's definitely the 'kiss and tell' type."

Maddie walked in, holding a little pup in her arms. As she caught the last part of the conversation, her smile vanished and she hugged the pup a little tighter. "See, I told you. All the girls at the camp said the same thing."

"That the puppy you told me about?"

Her smile returned and her eyes sparkled. "Want to hold him? He's so soft." She handed me the puppy, who immediately started sucking on my fingers. We all laughed.

Mrs. Chantilly was all smiles again and Melina took a turn at holding the pup before returning her to Maddie. The puppy was black and reminded me of a Labrador.

"Any idea what kind of dog? Or how big she'll get?"

"The mama is a Labrador, so she's at least part Lab. Some of the other pups look more like Labs, some look shorter in the legs. Some are brown with black markings, some black like her. So some kind of Lab mix."

"She has the shorter legs and the smoothest coat. And she's the smallest. Her mama is only a little bigger than Charlie." Maddie added.

Mrs. Chantilly chuckled. "The mama weighs about 50 lbs and that's partly because she was malnourished when she was found and brought here. I'm guessing that's about twice the weight of Charlie?" I nodded and she continued.

"The pups are about 4 weeks old and most of them are weighing between 8-10 lbs – typical for a Lab. This one here…" and she pointed to the squirming pup in Maddie's arms "weighed in this morning at 6 lbs. We started bottle-feeding her in addition to whatever she gets from mama the beginning of the week. But yeah, she'll probably grow to be a lot bigger than Charlie. On the other hand, Labs are great dogs with easy temperaments. Mama is probably stressing out that her pup is gone."

Maddie took the pup and went back to the side room. I helped Melina with a few more dogs and then dragged Maddie away from the puppies. Thankfully, I had hand sanitizer in my purse and we made our way to Al's. The selection was limited to sandwiches or burgers, but the food was good and the milkshakes to die for. To top it off, they had good coffee.

We ordered and Maddie was still talking about the puppy, when she suddenly stopped talking. I followed her gaze to a young girl walking with the help of a walker. She and an adult I assumed to be her mother moved in our direction. I glanced over to Maddie and she didn't say anything. She slid over to the chair next to mine as they reached our table.

"Hi Karla, Mrs. Champlin. This is my step-mom, Sheridan. Sheridan, this is Alex's sister, Karla, and his mother, Mrs. Champlin." Maddie nodded, proud of herself for her impeccable introduction.

I nodded and waved to the empty seats. "Please."

"Pleased to meet you, Mrs. McMann." I didn't bother to correct her on my name.

Karla moved her walker to the side and out of the way as she sat down. Now I understood what Melina meant when she said Alex helped with Karla. Other than the walker though, she seemed quite capable. Blonde with blue eyes, she was slim and dressed in capris and a t-shirt.

Mrs. Champlin nodded and smiled. She looked tired, her eyes puffy and bloodshot. "Yes, it's nice to meet you both. I've heard a lot about both of you from Karla and Alex. Have you ordered yet?"

"We have, but only a few minutes ago. Take your time." Maddie opened her mouth, and I put my hand on hers. "Give them a few minutes. The waitress is coming this way." Maddie slumped in her seat and waited.

Orders taken, Mrs. Champlin looked from Karla to Maddie, but didn't say a word. The silence was awkward. I cleared my throat. "Any updates? Maddie is worried about Alex."

Karla took Maddie's hand and Mrs. Champlin took a deep breath. "Chief Peabody told us to come by the station around 2 p.m. He said he hoped to have more information by then. If not, we'll at least be able to visit with Alex."

"Have they given you any idea what might happen next? I'm afraid I'm not up on Virginia law."

"He's in detention and they have to make a decision today to either keep him over the weekend or release him in my custody. His hearing would be on Monday, regardless. The court gave me the name of a lawyer just in case. There's no way he stole any money or killed that man. They have to figure it out. They have to."

She teared up and Karla leaned over and gave her a hug. "They will."

Maddie echoed Karla's assurances. "Anyone who knows Alex will figure out he was set up. Marty, a lawyer friend from in Cold Creek, is going to send Sheridan the name of a lawyer who may be able to help and Sheridan is real good at solving mysteries."

"I hope I'm not being nosy, but what do you do, Mrs. McMann?" Mrs. Champlin's knitted brows conveyed her confusion with Maddie's comment.

"Please call me Sheridan. I was on the faculty at Cold Creek College in the Psychology Department until I married Maddie's dad and moved up here with them. Right now, I'm looking to get back to teaching. Marty is a friend of ours – he's a lawyer and he said he'd try to find someone who specialized in juvenile cases up here."

Mrs. Champlin nodded. "Please call me, Angie. And the 'mysteries' she mentioned? I didn't quite understand that though Alex mentioned it as well."

"Over the last couple of years, I managed to find myself involved in police investigations. Not planned at all." Shifting the conversation, I added, "I understand you're a nurse? May I ask what you specialize in?"

"I'm trained as a surgical nurse; but those positions are few and far between. Right now I work in the Emergency Room. Pays about the same, but the hours can be longer."

The two of us continued to chat about work stuff and the two girls engaged in an animated conversation. A few times, I heard "puppy" and names of some of the dogs, so I knew Maddie was talking about our morning at Pets and Paws.

Food eaten, I picked up the check. "Allow me. The way these two are getting on, I'm sure we'll do this again."

Angie squirmed a little, her lips tight. To smooth it over, I added, "I'll take care of it this time and you can take care of it the next time, okay?"

She smiled. "In that case, okay. Nice to meet you. Come on, Karla."

Maddie grabbed Karla's walker and we all walked out together. I had the feeling we were being watched.

Turning around fast, I collided with Maddie as I scanned the restaurant. Only a fair-haired man, hiding behind a newspaper, sat by himself.

CHAPTER 7

Maddie was in a better mood and still excited about the puppy, which she'd already named Bella. I laughed, but also warned her it might not happen. She chattered on and on about Karla and Alex as well.

"We don't know what they're going to find out this afternoon. Don't get your hopes up too much. Legal stuff often moves in slow motion."

She grimaced in response to my warning. At home, she shot me a look with eyes sparkling and proceeded to get out of the car and walk to the house in slow motion. Well, she got as far as she could before she burst out laughing.

Inside, the first thing she asked was "What now? I don't have anything to do."

I said the first thing that came to my mind. "How about if you see what you can find out about the Buchanan and Stories families. A little history of the town?"

"You mean help you solve the murder mystery?"

"No. Neither of us has lived here very long and it might be good to learn the history and who's who."

"Okay. I'll see what I can find. I'm also gonna look up how to train a puppy and Labs." She leaned down to Charlie and ruffled her ears. "Charlie, you want a new playmate, right? You can teach Bella what dog life is all about." She disappeared into the study, Charlie at her heels and wanting more loving.

**

The phone ringing interrupted my thoughts and dinner preparation. It was Marty.

"So what's new with Maddie and her friend?"

"I'm not sure. Chief Peabody told his mother to come to the station at 2 o'clock for an update. We haven't heard anything since."

"Well, I have the information for a friend of mine up there – Eric Pinsky. He's good and specializes in juvenile cases. He does some pro-bono work and often is court appointed. For whatever reason, not many of us get involved in the juvenile side much. Lee's brother was a bit of a problem and Lee got to experience what the process was and how flawed it can be as a teen. He says that's why he's always allotted about 25 percent of his time to juvenile cases."

"So, sort of like you and trying to help your nephew, only younger?"

"That's about the size of it. But juvenile justice doesn't follow the same rules all the time and the process can be a lot more traumatic, especially if the kid is innocent."

"Thanks for the contact. I'll pass it on to Angie. Anything new down there since yesterday?"

"Nope, not really. I have to go pick up Kim for dinner, but stay in touch. I hope everything works out for Maddie and her friend."

I wrote down the name he'd given me and quickly looked up his website. A nice looking man sitting at a picnic table with teens was the banner. His credentials were off to the side along with the types of cases he usually accepted, including juvenile cases. I wrote down the URL for the site to pass on to Angie.

Dinner in the oven, I wondered if Maddie had fallen asleep. Charlie had rejoined me some time earlier, gone out, and slept in her bed. But not a peep from Maddie. Deciding to let her be, I had the table almost set when she barreled into kitchen area.

"Sheridan, Alex called. He's at home, but he doesn't know what's going to happen next. He has to go back on Monday. He sounded so tired and tense."

"That's to be expected, but think positive here. They didn't detain him over the weekend. He's home and he can rest up and meet with an attorney. Maybe by Monday, they'll have figured out who really killed Mr. Stories and stole the money."

"I sure hope so."

"What did you find out about the Buchanans?"

She didn't get a chance to answer as Brett pulled in the driveway as I finished speaking. Maddie didn't waste any time giving him a hug, offering to get him a cup of coffee, and telling him how glad she was to see him. Brett looked over to me with brows raised. I chuckled and shrugged.

"Daddy, did you have a busy day? You look a little stressed. I bet if you sit here and pet Charlie you'll feel better. I read about it on the Internet. Pet therapy they called it."

He sat down, his expression shifting between humor and suspicion of what was to come. I joined him at the table and enjoyed my cup of coffee as I watched Maddie's theatrics unfold.

Maddie used a hand signal and Charlie came over. "Daddy, did you see that? I didn't have to say a word and Charlie came. Dogs are easy to train, and they're good for you, help you relax, and I forget the other words they used to say how they helped people feel better."

"Now we love Charlie…" Maddie hesitated to scruff behind Charlie's ears. "But maybe Charlie would like company. I think Bella would be great company and Charlie and I will both train Bella. I'd take good care of her. Mom never let me have a dog, you know."

By the time she was through, Maddie directed her own puppy dog eyes at Brett. He wiped his hand across his face and glanced at me again.

"I guess you had a good time at Pets and Paws today, huh?"

Maddie bounced in her chair as she told him about the puppies and feeding Bella. His eyes twinkled and his mouth twitched as he figured out where this was going. When he discussed the responsibility, she stopped bouncing and listened. He kept looking to me for help.

"I told Maddie it was up to you and Charlie. Dogs are a lot of responsibility. We'd have to make sure Charlie and Bella got along." Of course, every time someone said her name, Charlie's tail wagged and she moved to the person speaking.

"We'll take it under consideration. No decisions yet." Maddie was about to start in on him again, when the oven timer sounded. Saved by the bell.

CHAPTER 8

As we cleared the table, I shifted the conversation. "So Maddie, what did you find out about the history of the town of Appomattox and the Buchanan family?"

"The Appomattox River was named after the Appamatuk Indians, though there were other names for them too. The town and the county were named after the river. Where's the river, Daddy?"

"It's north and east of the town of Appomattox, and flows to the south and east. It goes through the Appomattox-Buckingham State Forest. That's the largest state forest and Holiday Lake Park is there. Lots of hiking and horse trails."

His face lit up. "We might want to take a drive down there some time. It eventually passes south of Richmond and connects with Lake Chesdin. I think we went there once when you were little, Maddie. A popular place to visit is the Petersburg area, where they have lots of water activities, like kayaking, and hiking trails. It would be a fun long weekend, for sure." His eyes twinkled and his dimples showed. We'd definitely be going there, the only question was when.

"For sure. I think we've done all the hiking and biking trails in Appomattox and Clover Leaf." She hesitated and scrunched her face. "Daddy, what happened to the Indians?"

"They disappeared, Maddie. They moved away. I'm not sure, but I think it was before the Civil War."

"Now, I learned about the Civil War in school. I found a lot about the Civil War and how it ended right here in Appomattox with Lee's surrender. Sheridan, have you been to the historical park? There's lots to see and sometimes they have special events. We visited a couple times after Daddy moved here." She nodded and Brett smiled.

"Not yet, but I'll check the calendar and maybe you can show me around?" I wasn't sure when the park would be open again or if dogs were allowed. We'd only ventured to the small park in the neighborhood with Charlie, and there only once. For sure, though, if there was a special event about the Civil War, we'd have to invite Kim and Marty.

"That'd be fun. There were no mentions of Buchanans in the Civil War on either side, only a Wilmer McLean. MaryJane's last name is McLean. Do you think she's related to him?"

I shrugged. My knowledge of the Civil War didn't include him. Brett smiled and responded, "It's possible, but McLean is a common name."

"I bet not as common around here as Buchanan. There's some mention of Buchanan right after the Civil War. It looked like two brothers fought in the confederacy and ended up settling in the area right after the war ended, right here where Lee surrendered. The brothers married and were in farming, cotton, and building. They each had eight sons and their sons had sons and they spread out from here to settle in northern towns."

"Well, that is a little more detailed than what Mrs. Chantilly and Melina shared at Pets and Paws. From one generation to the next to go from two to sixteen? Wow. Melina mentioned a Blake Buchanan. Did you read about him?"

As Maddie talked, I noticed Brett was no longer smiling. In fact, he grimaced and drew his hand through his curls.

"Blake Buchanan was Mayor back several years – what does a mayor do, anyway? Are Luke and Caleb related to him? If so, he would be their grandfather I think cause he's old."

Brett cleared his throat. "Blake Buchanan was pretty influential here in Clover Leaf and he was Mayor of Appomattox for several years. Mayors make decisions about things in the town, like schools and roads. The Buchanan family is very large and they have a lot of clout in the county as well. There's one or two in politics elsewhere in the state, too."

Charlie barked and scratched at the door. "Maddie, how about you go outside with Charlie while it's still light and play with her."

"Come on, Charlie. Let's get your Frisbee."

After she left, the silence was deafening. "How bad are the Buchanans?"

"They have a lot of influence and money. The combination is power."

"Have you had any run-ins with them since you moved to Appomattox?"

Brett hesitated before he answered. "Nothing big. At least I didn't think it was big. Blake's youngest, Shane Buchanan, lives in the northeast part of the county. Married, two sons. I think one is in high school, one maybe about Maddie's age. Big house. He flaunted his wealth in contrast to the poverty in some of the nearby areas."

"He is the head honcho for the family's horse racing endeavor up there. Gambling and violations, allegations of mistreatment of the horses, and some protestors. It was a mess and the State Police got involved. I didn't like his attitude and he didn't like me. In the end, it was all resolved with some changes to how he did business. No big deal."

He shrugged, but if it occurred to me setting Maddie up could be payback, I was sure it occurred to him. I knew Brett often took cases a distance from Clover Leaf and the town of Appomattox. That was how we'd met.

"Mrs. Chantilly made a comment about the horses and the family's power. Is that going to be an issue with this murder case? One of their own?"

"Yes and no. Stories isn't a Buchanan. He's only related by law, not blood. How adamant they are the killer be punished to the highest extent of the law? No idea. On the other hand, if a Buchanan is the killer, or they think that's the case, they'll close ranks and do their best to shift the blame."

"You mean, to someone like Alex?"

"Yes." He shifted to glance outside and then continued. "Later."

He picked up my cup and his for a refill just as Maddie bounded in with Charlie behind her. Maddie plopped into a chair and Charlie made a beeline for her water bowl, tracking dirt as she went. Maddie shrugged. "We were playing with the Frisbee and she got into the garden to get it. Plants are all good."

I looked at her shorts and tee. Charlie wasn't the only one in the dirt. "Looks like you get to comb out Charlie and then get yourself cleaned up." Brett nodded as he reached over and wiped some dirt off her cheek.

Maddie made quick work of cleaning up Charlie and disappeared to create her own magic. I looked at Brett expectantly.

"The thing is they don't have enough to even hold Alex, never mind convict him of anything. Chief Peabody is beside himself and worried about the fallout. When it comes down to it though, he acknowledges all the evidence so far is circumstantial. Even the theft at the school doesn't stick because the money they found wasn't the money that was stolen."

"Is it possible the admin miscounted the money?"

"She's sure it was only $200 and it wasn't in an envelope. She also said it was all twenties, right from the ATM. What was in the envelopes wasn't new twenties. No, the money they found in Alex's pack – and in Maddie's – wasn't the pizza money."

"Where does that leave Alex and Maddie and the money? Who stole the pizza money?"

"With what is believed to be drug traces in the envelope, it leaves them in worse trouble than if they stole the pizza money. The good thing is, given the anonymous tip about the pizza money, even the chief thinks it was a set up. He did warn me to stay out of it until Maddie was cleared." He shook his head and ran his hand through his hair again. Here he was, in law enforcement, and not able to do what he did best – investigate.

"Okay, so what about Stories? Do they still think Alex killed him?"

"That's what really gets the Chief. Again, the only tie in, other than the money envelopes is the gun in the dumpster and an anonymous call telling them where it was. Alex doesn't live anywhere near the park. Without the call, they never would have checked the dumpster in his neighborhood."

He paused and smiled. "Besides, he has the best alibi around. He was in detention until 5. When the police brought him home, a nosy neighbor showed up at the house and she was still there when they came back and arrested him the second time. She says he never left the house. Even if he could have snuck out or if she's lying, there was no blood on his clothes.

And he hadn't changed since the morning. He's off the hook for the murder unless he's a magician."

"Well, that's good news. But both kids still potentially have a problem with what might be drug money?"

He nodded. We both sat in silence for a few minutes, broken by Charlie's bounding back into the kitchen, Maddie fast behind.

"Alex called again. He wants us to come over to his house for lunch tomorrow. His mom wants to pay us back for lunch today. Can we go Daddy, Sheridan? Please."

Brett's brows rose in question at her mention of lunch and I nodded.

"You get all the information, Maddie. Time and address, okay."

As she turned to bolt, I added, "And ask what we can bring." Then I told Brett about our lunch and meeting Angie and Karla.

CHAPTER 9

The morning passed by quickly, with time for a short walk with Charlie before leaving for lunch. A quick drive from Clover Leaf, Westerfield is more rural and older. The houses got closer together as we approached a small main street and turned onto Alex's street.

The house was an older ranch style with a touch of decorative trim. The outside was well kept, with lots of gardens. I spotted flowers, a large vegetable garden, and a few fruit trees. As we pulled up beside the older style SUV, three dogs of unknown breed and varying sizes came running from the back of the house. The door opened and a young man walked out and whistled. The three dogs immediately were at his feet. We needed him at Pets & Paws.

Maddie hopped out of the car all smiles and we followed.

"Hi Alex. Who are the dogs?"

The young man with blonde hair and blue eyes smiled at Maddie. "Duke, Duchess, and Joker." He pointed from the biggest to the smallest – maybe a mix between a Chihuahua and a terrier of some sort.

As we walked up the ramp to the porch, Alex turned to Brett and me and extended his hand, which Brett shook. "Hi. I'm Alex. Thanks for coming. Please come in."

Alex was taller than Maddie, on the slim side but stood straight and proud even with what he'd been through the last few days.

Introductions for Brett continued inside as we gathered around a small table in their kitchen. Angie smiled when Alex introduced Brett and then buzzed around the kitchen in jeans and tee shirt, her short blonde hair clipped back. She had prepared quite the spread with sandwiches, chips, salad, and fruit. I added the cupcakes we'd brought.

Conversation was between bites and mostly a repeat with Brett of the questions Angie had asked me. She seemed surprised when he revealed he was a detective with the State Police. Small talk and food done, Angie suggested the kids check the gardens for any fruit or vegetables that needed to be collected.

As I cleared my plate and put it in the sink, I stopped to watch Karla. She was using the walker and in charge of the basket for whatever they picked. Her wedge cut hair was long enough to swing from side to side as she walked. The biggest dog, Duke, stood next to her and moved with her, as if on guard.

"Beautiful gardens. Is Duke Karla's dog?"

"Yes, he was trained as a service dog for someone else. He's been with us now for about three years and around the yard he's always near her. He will become her walker if it tips over or sound an alarm if she needs help. It's important for her to be able to be outside and do as much as she can."

"That's great. And Duchess and Joker?"

She chuckled. "Strays, plain and simple. I think Duchess could be trained to be a service dog. She's pretty smart. Joker? Well, he's usually good for a laugh for some of his shenanigans – that is when he's not making a pest of himself. But with Karla? They're all very loyal and protective."

We sat down. "So Detective, what's going to happen next?"

"I'm Brett, not a detective here. Chief Peabody has made it clear because of Maddie and her connection to Alex." He looked at me and raised his brows. I shrugged and plunged in.

"Angie, are you aware someone also stuck envelopes with money in Maddie's backpack?"

"What? No, I only know what the police told me. They found the pizza money in Alex's backpack. They won't even give it back – the backpack I mean."

I glanced at Brett and it was his turn to shrug.

"The police were called to the school because the pizza money was stolen, yes. And they had a tip to check Alex and Maddie's packs. Once they found money in Alex's, they didn't check Maddie's but we did, at home. There was more money and the police have it now."

"Because of that, I can't be involved. Besides, it's not a State Police case any way. Nonetheless, I can tell you though most of the evidence against Alex is circumstantial for both theft and murder."

"That's what the attorney I talked to said. He thinks the charges will be dropped."

"Oh, you have an attorney? Our friend Marty called with a name in case you needed one."

"Well, I never met this man. He's the one the court told me to contact. Eric Pinsky. He seemed nice enough on the phone."

"He's the same person Marty recommended." I nodded in affirmation.

"Good. I…I don't have much experience in this stuff. It's hard to know who to trust."

I nodded. She opened her mouth, but closed it. She glanced out the window before she spoke.

"I don't know what will happen. Monday we go to court. I have to work and Alex will stay with my neighbor. He loved the camps and all he was learning, but …"

Brett leaned toward her. "We aren't letting Maddie go back either. Not until this is all resolved. Did Alex ever mention any of the other kids at the camps?"

She smiled. "He talked a lot about Maddie. Maddie did this. Maddie said this." She paused and the smile disappeared. "He also talked about some snobby girls and some older boys. I got the feeling there was some bullying go on though he never actually said."

Brett nodded. We talked a while longer and then joined the kids outside. Both Maddie and Alex would need showers for sure and not just from the heat, but the dirt. Karla was all smiles and egging the other two on.

"You about ready to go home, Maddie?"

Her shoulders slumped. "Do we have to go?"

"Yes, we do. We have errands to run and Charlie needs a walk. Ms. Champlin has things to do and I'm sure Karla and Alex have chores, too."

"That's right, laundry needs to get done and we promised Mrs. Daniels we'd make her an apple pie for the picnic tomorrow." Angie looked from Alex to Karla. They nodded. "Now, Alex grab a bag and put some of the fruit and vegetables in it for the McManns."

"That's not necessary, really. Thank you and thank you again for lunch."

She ignored me and we left with a bag of fruit and vegetables. I liked Angie and hoped we'd be friends when this was all over.

CHAPTER 10

I woke up to the smell of coffee brewing and sizzling bacon. A good day for sure, I thought. Until I ventured to the kitchen and Brett turned toward me with scowl on his face.

"Smells good. Why the scowl?"

He shook his head, turned the stove off, and tilted his head to the garage. I followed, not quite sure what he had in mind.

He closed the door to the kitchen and took a deep breath before he spoke. "I got up early to get a quick run in before it got too hot. I found this box…" He pointed to a nondescript brown shipping box.

"On the front step. Almost tripped over it. It's addressed to Maddie."

I started to open the box and he stopped me. "You don't need to look. Inside is a dead rat, a joint, and a note with 'watch out' in block letters. I called Chief Peabody and he's going to stop by a little later."

I gasped and pulled him to me. His hands shook and he gripped me in a tight hug as he pulled himself together. "Come on. Let's try to keep things normal and finish getting breakfast cooked."

I nodded. As he prepared the eggs and toast, I set the table. I washed and cut up some of the fruit we'd brought back from the Champlin's and made a fruit salad. As usual, Maddie slept through it all, leaving Brett and I to eat alone.

"Any thoughts?"

"How about you and Maddie go on a bike ride? Or take Charlie for a walk? I don't want her hanging around when Peabody gets here."

"That'd work." I thought back over what Maddie had told me about Caleb and Luke. "Did I tell you what Maddie said about Caleb? The way he had an odd sweet smell? Do you think it could be from smoking a joint? Isn't marijuana in that form still illegal, even for medicinal purposes?"

"Medical marijuana is legal for the oil form only right now, and not likely to give off the sweet smell. The smell, well, it could be from smoking pot or it may be a bad choice of cologne. Some of the men's stuff is pretty bad. I hope they…"

"Good morning." Maddie shuffled into the kitchen in her boxer-style pajamas and slid into her chair at the table. Charlie put her nose on Maddie's lap, hoping for a stray piece of bacon.

"Morning yourself. Have some orange juice, while I whip you up some eggs." Brett poured her juice and I slid the fruit salad in her direction.

"Did you have any plans for today? It's a beautiful day outside and not too hot yet." At her shrug, I continued, "Your dad mentioned cleaning out the garage. Maybe after you eat and get dressed, we'll take Charlie for a walk, maybe go for a short bike ride later on. What do you think?"

She nodded as she ate her fruit. In no time, her eggs were ready. As she ate, I started the clean up with furtive glances to Brett as he hovered a bit more than usual.

Timing is everything, and Maddie emerged from her room in shorts and tee shirt, hair braided at the same time Chief Peabody pulled in the driveway. I had Charlie haltered and leashed and she was ready for her adventure.

Maddie's smile disappeared when she saw the policeman. "What's he doing here again?"

"Probably talking business with your dad, following up on the money in your back pack, something official or he wouldn't be here on a Sunday morning. We'll let them be and take Charlie here for her walk, okay?"

"I guess." She fingered her braid. Charlie pawed at her and licked her hand. That got a chuckle out of her. "Okay, I get the message. Let's go. Do you have the baggies, Sher?"

I nodded and we were on our way. Brett had intercepted the chief outside the garage, and we exchanged the usual pleasantries as we set out on our walk around the neighborhood.

Ours was one of a group of condominiums in a

settled neighborhood. The greens around the eight condominiums were well groomed, though the heat of the summer had taken its toll in a few places where the sprinkler system didn't quite reach. The other residences were relatively newer construction, ranch style like the condos, and most had a few gardens and a tree or two in the front yard. Someone had spent time and money to ensure the condos matched the style of the existing homes and the same with the newest homes.

Brett had said the neighborhood was pretty much all families, however, I'd yet to meet many of the neighbors. With our condo on the end, our closest neighbors had gone on vacation soon after I moved in at the end of the school year. They were friendly in a polite way with younger children. This was only our second foray into the neighborhood with Charlie. There was a small neighborhood park and playground and that's where we headed.

It was starting to get warm and I was glad I'd brought water with us. We stopped by a bench and Maddie pulled out a collapsible bowl, garnered from the camping gear, to let Charlie have a drink. I looked around and noticed a few teens, probably Maddie's age, and a bench in the shade near some other adults.

We meandered in that general direction. The grass had just been cut and there was a sign directing people to "Frisbee Golf" I hadn't noticed the only other time we'd been here.

As if on cue, I heard "Watch out!" Probably the exact wrong thing to do, I turned toward the person yelling and immediately pulled Maddie to the side. Charlie saved the day as she jumped up and caught the Frisbee in the air. She sat with her tail wagging, Frisbee in her mouth, pleased with herself.

"Good girl, great catch." I looked up as a young man sauntered over, shaking his head.

"Sorry about that. I'm trying to teach my sister how to throw a Frisbee – preferably in the intended direction. Not working so far."

I felt Maddie tense up, but she was looking past the young man. A pretty girl, long blonde curls loosely tied back, walked toward us. She sported what reminded me of a golf outfit, with the Puma name displayed prominently. Her outfit accentuated her developing curves.

"Hi, MaryJane. This is Sheridan. She and my dad got married in June."

"Hello yourself, Maddie. This is my brother, Drew. He's the captain of the football team at Clover Leaf High."

"Nice to meet you and all, but can we get our Frisbee back now?" He glanced at his watch and then his sister. "We only have a little longer before we need to get back home for lunch."

His comment brought all the attention back to Charlie, still holding the Frisbee. "It's nice to meet you both as well. MaryJane, I think Maddie mentioned you from the camps. Drew do you attend the camps, too?"

"No, ma'am, I have football practice every day. The Frisbee?"

"Oh... Charlie, drop." Charlie complied and I picked up the Frisbee. "Here, let me wipe if off for you. She kind of slobbered all over it."

I looked around for something to use and Maddie handed me the paper towel she'd used to wrap Charlie's bowl. Drew shifted his balance from one foot to the other.

"So you're at the High School? You must know the two high school boys at camp with Maddie and MaryJane then."

Drew's eyebrows raised and jaw clenched, he turned to his sister. "You never mentioned any boys in high school only the one arrested for stealing the pizza money."

"Um, not important." MaryJane shrugged and reached for the Frisbee.

Maddie caught on and offered, "Luke and Caleb, right? They're both in high school, I think. No, never mind, they're going to the Academy, right MaryJane?"

MaryJane's face fell and color seeped up from her chest into her face. Her brother's face turned red much faster and he worked his jaw for a few seconds before he responded. "Yes, they are. MaryJane, I told you to steer clear of those Buchanans. They're nothing but trouble. Now come on or we'll be late for lunch."

I extended the now cleaned off and dry Frisbee. He nodded and walked away. Then he turned back. "Maddie? You stay away from those two, too." He glanced from Maddie to me and I nodded. Message received.

"Wow. He's cute."

"Yes, he is and he's obviously not a fan of Caleb and Luke. There are some other kids over there. Do you recognize any of them?"

Maddie stared in that direction for a while. "I can't tell. Can I take Charlie over there? I bet the girls will want to pet her and play with her."

I nodded and marveled at the draw of a dog as a means to make friends. Maddie had a point. If you're walking a dog, many more people will strike up a conversation. While I waited, I sat down and checked my phone for any messages from Brett. Hopefully, he'd give us an all clear on when we could go home. Nothing yet.

"Hello, are you new to the neighborhood? We don't recognize you, though Heather here thinks she recognizes the young girl." The brunette standing in front of me, flanked by two other women, sounded friendly, curious, and suspicious all at once. Her body language was stiff and her smile didn't meet her eyes.

"Yes, I'm new to the neighborhood. I'm Sheridan and the young girl is Maddie. Maddie's been visiting her dad here weekends for about two years now I think. She moved up here permanently sometime in April. Her dad and I were married in June and that's when I moved here."

"Welcome to the neighborhood then. I'm Kristen Brewer, this is Heather Hamilton. The pushy one is Ashley Jones." Kristen's smile was real and she beamed her welcome. Ashley relaxed a bit, no longer quite at attention. Heather was the youngest of the three and obviously pregnant.

"Nice to meet you. Heather, I hope you don't mind me asking – when are you due?"

"Not a problem, no way to hide my bundle of joy anymore. The doctor says I'm due in three weeks and that's not soon enough. We're here walking and hoping it speeds up Katie's arrival."

"I think that's a hint, Sheridan. It was nice meeting you and we hope to see more of you." Kristen smiled again, and the threesome walked on past me, Heather working hard to keep up.

Sitting on the bench, I pondered what we knew and didn't know. My thoughts were interrupted by the beep of my phone with the "all clear" from Brett. I stretched and walked toward the group of kids having a fun time with Charlie.

"Hi Sheridan. This is Nedra and these are all friends of hers who might be in my class. And Charlie here is a total hit."

"Nice to meet everyone. Maddie, do you remember Ms. Melina at Pets and Paws?"

Maddie nodded her head and Nedra chimed in, "She's my mom."

Maddie immediately started in on the puppies and everyone laughed at her descriptions of their antics. It took me a few minutes to get a happier Maddie pointed back toward home, with Charlie in tow.

.

CHAPTER 11

Brett was hard at work in the garage when we got home. Maddie quickly told him about the friends she made at the park. I took Charlie inside and got a bottle of water for Brett.

"What's the plan for today? Do we have one?"

"You said you hadn't been to the Historical Park, so one option is to go there and walk around. Is there anything you want to do or need to do? Shopping? Laundry? I should be through in here in about an hour. After lunch, we can do whatever you girls want."

"Maybe we could stop and see Bella at Pets and Paws? And then go to the park?" Maddie bounced as she asked.

Brett looked over at me and I chuckled. "I think there's a certain bedroom that needs to be cleaned up. And speaking of shopping, I've noticed some of your pants aren't fitting right – you're growing or the fabric is shrinking."

"I can totally clean my room and figure out which clothes don't fit any more. So, we can go after lunch?"

"Sounds like a plan." Brett conceded with a grin. "But you need to get to work on your room and help Sheridan with lunch."

Maddie dashed into the house and we moved as far from the door as possible before Brett shared his conversation with the chief.

He shook his head. "Peabody took the box, rat, and joint though he's not too sure there's any way to identify who sent it. He suggested Maddie go stay with her mother for a while."

Brett shook his head again and took a deep breath. "I told him Victoria and Roger were out of the country and they weren't likely to come back for Maddie. It got a little awkward there, but he got the picture." Their whole trip abroad for business reasons had been dumped on Maddie suddenly along with the decision she move in with Brett full time.

"What now?"

"They're still investigating the murder and the drug leads. I mentioned the 'sweet smell' and he nodded. My guess? He wouldn't be surprised in the least, but there's no evidence other than envelopes of money of any connection between the murder and drugs. Stories' prints weren't on the envelope."

"So somebody could have planted them with the body to confuse things?"

Brett shrugged. "You never can tell. If Stories was

into drugs – taking or dealing – Peabody didn't have or share that intel. I'd gotten the impression Stories supported anti-drug campaigns myself."

Brett continued to organize all the additional "stuff" that came with my move, while I cleaned up the kitchen and got lunch ready.

I heard Brett's phone and stuck my head into the garage to be sure he got it. He nodded. A few minutes later, he came in, his jaw set, and I knew it wasn't good news. I immediately thought of Alex and Maddie. Nothing even close.

"That call was from headquarters. They're short on manpower. I have to go to Hixburg in the morning, it's not clear if I'll have to stay there or be able to come home."

Hixburg was only 20 minutes away, maybe 30 in bad weather. "What's going on? Why would you need to stay over?"

"So far, there's no crime. Still, there are significant concerns there might be trouble and things could potentially get out of hand. The governor is concerned but doesn't want to go overboard. Mr. Barrymore Whistklan is scheduled to spout his beliefs. He and his friends like to stir things up. You know who he is, right?"

"Yes, one of those extremists. Talks a lot about every controversial topic to try and get people riled up, whether he believes it or not. That's him right?"

"It is and around here, with all the battles fought in the Civil War, the confederacy is an easy focus. The Civil War might have ended, but even generations later, the sentiments of the confederacy sometimes persist. Unfortunately, when Whistklan spouts, other groups feel a need to speak out in rebuttal. I don't understand why Hixburg allowed him to purchase a public forum, anticipating what would likely happen. He stirs up hate and people get hurt."

"We'll hope you can get home. Maybe other people will be smart enough not to show up. That would be the best option. If he didn't have an audience, he might shut up. Instead, he gets a lot of free publicity with his hate speech repeated over and over through the media."

He nodded and took me in his arms.

"Right now, let's have lunch and you can meet Bella. Have a seat and I'll go get Maddie. Hopefully, she's not too excited to eat."

***

Maddie chattered the entire drive to Pets and Paws, sharing everything she'd learned about the old house and the dogs, especially Bella. Sunday was always an open house, with the intent to encourage people to come adopt the residents.

There were a few cars in the parking lot and Mrs. Chantilly was helping a couple to their car with the new addition to their family, a beagle mix was my best guess. Mrs. Chantilly gave out baskets with food, toys, treats, and basic instructions for obedience training to help new owners. She joined us on the steps.

"Hello Sheridan, Maddie. You must be Mr. McMann. I'm Mrs. Chantilly. Please come in and Sheridan and Maddie can show you around." She was all smiles though obviously busy. She bustled over to a family playing with Razor.

"Come on, Daddy, this is the way to the new mamas and puppies." Maddie took his hand and I followed behind.

"This is where Bella is. See there's her mama, the chocolate lab. And the other pups are feeding. But where is Bella?" Maddie got down on the floor and started moving the puppies around, searching for Bella. More than one puppy climbed into her lap. Puppies rearranged, the littlest pup emerged and sought out mama.

"See her, Daddy. She's the runt and not so big as the others who get all the food. Susie and I feed her some with a bottle 'cause she can't get to mama as easy as these guys."

Susie joined us. "Maddie's right. The little one had a bottle a little while ago, but she is always hungry."

"How're the adoptions going with the mamas and pups?"

"This one here – we call her "Brown Sugar" from her coloring and her puppies? We have commitments from fosters or forever homes for six of the eight puppies. The biggest and the littlest aren't placed yet. They won't be able to go anywhere for another week or so, until after we get them weaned and dewormed. We're working on a foster for Brown Sugar, but puppies go much faster than the mamas."

Susie continued talking to update the status on the other two mamas and pups. They were all a few weeks ahead of Brown Sugar and her family.

While Susie was talking, Maddie extricated herself from the litter. As soon as Bella moved off her mama, Maddie picked her up. "Daddy, you have to hold her. She is so soft and gentle. I don't think she's going to get very big."

He took the puppy and with his 6-foot plus frame, the pup looked very small. "Maddie, she's a lab, and her mama isn't so little. In all likelihood, with good food and care, this pup may end up as big as her. Puppies are cute, but they grow up to be dogs."

Her smile faded, if only for a minute. "I know, like Charlie. And Mrs. Chantilly guessed she'd be bigger than Charlie when she was full grown. But, Daddy, she's so cute. Can't we take her, maybe at least foster her?"

He chuckled. "We'll think on it. You know who will have the final say, don't you?"

She exhaled. "Sheridan already told me. Charlie. When can we bring her over to meet Bella?"

I looked over to Susie. "Not until the pups are a little older and we can easily move them away from Brown Sugar without her getting agitated. She's very protective still."

Maddie took Bella back from Brett and cuddled her. I wasn't sure if she even noticed Brown Sugar never took her eyes off the pup.

"Okay, how about the rest of this tour and then we can enjoy the Historical Park?"

Maddie gave Bella back to her mama, who immediately took to cleaning the pup and made us all laugh. The tour was short, though it was obvious to me Brett gravitated to the bigger dogs and relaxed more when he interacted with them than with the small puppy. Melina and her daughter, Nedra arrived as we were leaving with introductions all around.

***

It was a short drive from Pets and Paws to the park. Brett asked a lot of questions about Mrs. Chantilly and the dogs. I explained she had the history of Pets and Paws posted.

"An interesting story, really. She inherited the house from her grandmother who loved dogs and always took in strays. The property came to her with about 10 dogs of varying sizes and shapes, along with some damage from having many dogs over the years."

"I would imagine there'd be damage and the smell…"

"Yup. She decided to honor her grandmother and follow her lead. She updated the bottom floor, staining the floors for easier maintenance. Dogs had never been upstairs and she moved in there. She loves the dogs and is well off so it's not like she needs to make money."

"There are worse hobbies or passions. Glad someone takes care of these strays."

"Me, too. There is something odd about her, though. I can't put my finger on it." I gave it more thought as we made our way to the park.

The easiest way to get to the park was a road with lots of construction on the side and a soft shoulder, with ditches dug for who knows what. I'd no sooner commented on that and I heard Brett swear under his breath. I looked past him and saw a car coming up along side us.

Thankfully, nobody was coming toward us we could see, though the double white line indicated a no passing zone. Next thing I knew, the car angled toward us, not having cleared our car. Only Brett's good reflexes kept us on the road and out of the ditch. The other car sped off.

"Maddie, you okay back there?" He'd looked over to me and I'd nodded before he spoke.

"Yes. But what happened? Didn't they see us?"

Brett took a deep breath. "I'm not sure Maddie." He looked at me before he opened his door. "Sit tight. I'm going to see if there's any damage."

I watched him in the side view mirror as he pulled out his phone. The car hadn't hit us so the only damage would be if we had a flat tire or were hung up on something.

"No damage and we should be able to get back on the road without any problem." He managed to get us back on the road with ease. When we reached the Park, he pulled a notebook out from under his seat. "While it's still fresh in your mind, I want you to write down anything and everything you remember about the car that tried to…uh, pass us." As I opened my mouth, he shook his head. "Don't say it out loud. Just write it down. Please."

A few minutes later we entered the park. We visited the McLean House and we were able to walk around the village on the West side. We weren't able to see the East side where two roads intersected. That section and the cabin at that site were closed off.

I looked at Brett and he nodded. That was where Stories had been murdered. Hot and tired, we picked up information on the trails and upcoming events before heading home.

CHAPTER 12

The ride home was quiet and uneventful other than Maddie falling asleep in the back seat. Brett and I decided it was a good night for burgers and hot dogs. We made a quick stop at the grocery store and picked up what we needed.

At home, Maddie took Charlie outside for some Frisbee, talking to her the whole time about how much she'd like Bella. Brett got the grill going and we waited for the meat to cook. In the meantime, Brett studied the observations we'd each written down.

He shook his head. "The problem and plus of eye witness testimony is no two people remember what happened exactly the same. The only thing we agree on is the car was a goldish brown – what you and I labeled as titanium. You and I agree it was like an

Accord, same size as your car or mine. No surprise, Maddie saw it as bigger than either of our cars. I didn't notice the driver and I'm ashamed to say I didn't get the license plate. Maddie noticed someone in the passenger seat. She wrote she saw 'a head above the head rest and big shoulders. A fat man.' Did you notice that?"

"Sorry, when I thought he was trying to pass us, I kept looking for a car to be coming in the other direction around the curve."

"But you said 'he.' Did you see something that made you think a man?"

I shook my head. "No. I assume someone pulling out like that to pass would be male, not female."

He nodded. "I don't think the intent was to pass us. They came up fast behind us as soon as we hit the construction area. They wanted us in the ditch." His jaw was tight and he clenched the pencil he held so tight, it snapped.

"So what now?"

"I notified both Chief Peabody and my boss about the incident, but we don't have any way to identify them. Though I'm thankful I avoided a direct hit – which would have landed us in the ditch – there's nothing to trace. No paint chips or damage to their car to help locate it. And that color mid-size car is pretty common."

"True enough." I jumped up to grab my phone as the standard ring tone sounded.

"Hi, Melina."

"Hi, Sheridan. After you left, Nedra made some comments about Luke and Caleb. She heard from friends of hers about Luke and some other boy having a run in and it had to do with Maddie. She couldn't remember the other boy's name, but her friends? They all figured Luke would get even somehow with both of them. I asked her what else she knew about Luke and Caleb. She shrugged and said 'trouble with a capital T' and then hesitated to add rumors they were dealing drugs."

"Did she say anything else about Maddie or the drugs?"

"Not really. She said her friends were glad somebody stood up to those two. Nedra was glad to hear Maddie would be in the same school this fall. Hopefully, they can get to know each other in the next few weeks before school starts."

"That'd be great. Thanks for calling, Melina. We'll see you tomorrow."

I relayed the gossip to Brett, which led to discussion of Monday. "She wants to go the detention hearing in the morning. Should she go back to camp? Ever? Can you get your money back?"

He raked his hands through his curls. "Not back to camp until this is figured out. If you can go with her to the hearing, that's okay. I don't really care whether we get the money back from the camps or not. If this is resolved quickly, she'd have maybe three or four weeks left, right?"

"Possibly. We'll go to the hearing and then to Pets and Paws. She'll like that and I can run errands or such while she's playing with the dogs. Any new information on Stories' murder? What did Stories do anyway?"

"Stories got a business degree and he was owner and CEO of a consulting firm. He or his firm, now his wife, Lila, mostly got involved when companies were down-sizing or in financial straits. Not quite like the guy in *Pretty Woman*, but close. Stories would help them figure out who to lay off and how to best deal with severance. Stories didn't actually buy businesses out. He found someone else who was willing to invest in whatever the company did or wanted to buy them out to get rid of competition. He was a broker of sorts."

"So, wait. Any of those companies or their employees might have a motive for murdering him?"

"Not quite. It's highly unlikely individual employees would be aware of Stories' role. There's no indication he ever interacted with the employees, only management. There's also no indication he or his company ever received any threats or complaints."

"What else, then?"

"He advocated for women's rights, for one thing. When he worked with a company, he insisted on equitable conditions and equal pay, as well as equal likelihood of being laid off. He talked at the police academy once, gave an invited presentation on the rights of women historically and in the present. He made several points related to unequal pay and inequities in assignments that had nothing to do with ability, but were all about gender. It was tense and awkward when he asked one person in the audience to tell him the name of the male officer next to him and then the female officer. He pointed out the difference in whether last or first name was used. He was eloquent and didn't pull any punches."

"Do you really think those views could get someone killed?"

"No. He made people think and reflect. He was not an agitator like Whistklan." Brett shrugged. "Peabody said they are investigating all avenues from drugs to money to a crossed lover."

"He was cheating on his wife?"

"Not that anyone can find, but that would certainly be a motive if he was, no matter how discreet he might have been."

"Anything else?

"Some talk he might get into politics, try to change policy and law. Not sure that could get him killed either. For one thing, he'd have to get elected first. From what I got out of Peabody, Stories wasn't always in good graces with the Buchanans, other than his wife, Lila. Stories was sometimes very vocal in public meetings. Clearly, his allegiance was not with the confederacy and he took issue with the power the NRA seems to have right now. So politically, he wasn't on same page as the Buchanans. He also would make comments about how Lila was disrespected and ignored by her family because she was a girl even though she's smarter than her brothers."

"That still doesn't seem like a motive for murder. More like a reason not to invite somebody for dinner."

"Apparently, his not getting invited to a dinner provided another opportunity for him to complain about his in-laws. And although they all were part of the same country club crowd, Stories didn't hesitate to insult Shane Buchanan or Luke in public. The more I hear about Luke, the more I think I need to have a heart to heart with that young man. And unlike the Buchanans, the Stories boys attend Clover Leaf High, not Clover Hill Academy."

"Huh. You're probably right about Luke, but let's get this resolved first. If Luke is involved, you don't want to put a target on Maddie's back. What about Lila?"

"Lila? She got her degree in business as well and works – worked – with Stories. She will take over as the CEO now he's gone. Because of the family feelings of where women belong, she's been the silent partner all along. Blake Buchanan will not be happy when the partnership is no longer silent. They had three sons. The oldest is in the Navy. The other two are in high school and work part-time in the business. They all seem to keep a low profile despite being in a high profile family."

.

CHAPTER 13

After a tense breakfast, we set off for the courthouse and Brett set off for Hixburg. At the courthouse, security was pretty quick and we followed the signs. Karla was seated alone on a bench and we joined her.

"Good morning. How are you this morning, Karla?"

"Where's Alex and your mom?"

"They're in there for the hearing. Nobody else can go in. I'm scared."

We sat down on either side of Karla. "We'll wait with you if that's okay."

She nodded and Maddie added, "Yeah and then it won't be so scary."

After a few minutes of silence, Maddie asked after their dogs and launched into her sales pitch for Bella. I watched as different people in suits or uniforms, mostly male, walked past with side glances at us, or went into various doors on the hallway. Another small group sat further down the hallway.

The doors opened and a tall, stocky young man emerged in a sports shirt and pressed jeans, with a man in a suit who was almost as tall. The young man was nodding at whatever the suit was telling him. I heard Maddie gasp and turned to her. She shook her head and then turned sideways to face Karla so she wasn't facing the duo. The young man and the suit walked away.

"That was Caleb. Caleb Buchanan," Maddie whispered.

Karla nodded. "He's big and mean."

"Has he ever been mean to you, Karla?"

She shook her head and then stopped. "He makes comments about me and my walker, but not to me, exactly. I only know because a friend told me. Her brother is the same age as Caleb. They go to the same church. Her brother is nice and helps me sometimes."

"That's good. It's important for all of us to know there are people to help us."

"Yeah, like Alex helped me with Luke."

A few minutes later, Angie, Alex, and a man walked out the door. The man was of medium height and his suit didn't hide his athletic build. I recognized Pinsky from his website. Taller than Angie and Alex, he continued to speak with the two of them as the door closed behind them. Alex pointed toward us, and they all came in our direction.

Karla stood up and Alex gave her a hug. "It's

okay."

Angie introduced us to Eric Pinsky as friends of the family.

"Nice to meet you Mr. Pinsky. Marty Cohn mentioned your name, in a positive manner of course."

"Marty's a good friend and colleague. He has mentioned you and some of your involvement down in Cold Creek before." He winked with a smile and shook my hand.

Maddie, who'd been fidgeting, stopped. "So what happened? Is Alex free?"

Pinsky cleared his throat and looked to Angie. She nodded.

"At this point there is not sufficient evidence to prove Alex had anything to do with the theft of the pizza money or the murder of Mr. Stories. Mrs. Daniels's testimony was a big help. He is free to go while the investigation continues."

Karla and Maddie squealed. I caught the undertones and implications. Both cases were still open, so this wasn't a "get out of jail free card" for Alex or Maddie. Pinsky hadn't mentioned Caleb's role at all. At Angie's suggestion, we decided to meet for lunch. They had one stop to make to complete paperwork, and we left.

As we walked out of the building, I saw movement at the corner. The sun cast an eerie shadow of a person on the side of the building, an obviously distorted image, getting wider as the shadow extended onto the grass. We continued walking and I kept my eye on the shadow. When the shadow moved forward as if to follow us, I turned and looked. It was a middle aged man with fair hair. Realizing I had spotted him, he turned and walked in the other direction. Creepy.

Lunch was good, more relaxed than before. I was curious about Caleb and asked, "Maddie pointed out Caleb as he left the court. What was he doing there?"

Pinksy coughed. "He was the one who found the… Stories. He was testifying to how he came to find the body."

"He was confused and kept looking to his attorney and toward the back of the room. Mr. Pinsky, did you notice it? Does he have a disability?"

Pinsky shrugged. "I don't know much about him, never met him. I was surprised his parents weren't there, only the attorney. The two of them were talking to another man outside of the courthouse earlier. Could have been his father."

"Maddie, Alex, is Caleb usually like Mrs. Champlin described?"

Alex answered. "Sometimes he doesn't respond at all and looks like he's about to fall asleep. I'm not sure if I'd call him confused."

"And he's clumsy and smells funny."

Pinsky smiled at Maddie's comment and we talked about afternoon plans. After lunch, I took Maddie to Pets and Paws. Melina agreed to keep an eye on her, so I ran errands. She suggested Maddie go to their house for dinner so the girls could become better acquainted. I agreed. As I left Pets and Paws, I had the feeling I was being watched. Across the street I spotted a man who looked like the one at the courthouse. He turned away so I didn't see his face. I wondered why he was following us.

***

I hung up the phone and bounced in place, much like Maddie. Silly, for an adult, but I was excited. My next instinct was to call Kim.

"Hi, Kim, you got a few minutes?"

"What's up? It must be good news – your voice is high." Kim chuckled.

"A Dr. Addison called from Millicent College. One of their faculty members in psychology is taking family medical leave and they need someone to fill in next year."

"Great! When's the interview?"

"Tomorrow. They'd like to have the person in place in enough time for the start of the fall semester."

"Have you ever heard anything about Millicent College? Where is it?"

"It's a private liberal arts college in Lynchburg. Small psychology department, but good reputation. About 30 minutes from here I think."

"That's great, Sheridan. It will at least keep you out of trouble. I sure hope you didn't list Max as a reference. He'll warn them to watch out for dead bodies if they hire you."

We both laughed. "No, I didn't list him. Anything new with him?"

"Not really. He's acting like he'll be the new

department head sooner rather than later, strutting around and giving orders. Allie and Terra put him straight every time and then he sulks away. I hope they find someone else, even hire someone from the outside."

"For sure. Brett's pulling in the driveway, so I'm going to get off the phone and tell him the good news. I'll call you tomorrow after the interview."

Putting the phone down, I rushed to meet Brett at the door, glad he was able to get home. My mood deflated when I saw how exhausted he looked. Obviously, he had a much less positive day than I.

He pulled me into his arms. "There was a time I loved being on the streets. Must be getting old, but I definitely prefer the detective side of things. Angry crowds. Speaker intentionally agitating the crowds and inciting those who agreed with him to take on those who didn't. Why? What does that do except make for a lot more work to keep everyone safe. Thankfully, it broke up quickly and didn't get out of control. Nowhere near as bad as the governor envisioned."

"Take a shower, get changed, and then you can tell me about it."

He nodded and walked away. Turning around, he asked, "Where's Maddie? It's awfully quiet."

"She was at Pets and Paws all afternoon. Melina invited her to dinner at their house to hang out with Nedra. I said it was okay. We're supposed to pick her up around 8 o'clock unless Maddie calls to come home sooner."

"Good. Okay. Shower."

By the time Brett returned, some of the stress in his face and shoulders alleviated, I had pulled together a quick dinner. With Maddie gone, I added a glass of wine for each of us.

"Tell me about your day – I suspect you will see most of what mine was like on the news."

"Court, then Pets and Paws for a while and mostly hanging around here." I smiled and he tilted his head.

"You're smiling like a Cheshire cat, yet 'hanging around' isn't your usual favorite thing to do. Should I be worried?"

"Nothing to worry about. At least I don't think so. I have an interview tomorrow for a job at Millicent College!"

He smiled. "That's great, Sher. A toast to you and your interview." We clinked our glasses.

"Will you do the same thing as what you did at Cold Creek?"

"Teaching, yes. Administrative stuff, definitely not. It's a one year visiting position, at least for now. And Millicent's Psychology Department is much smaller than Cold Creek's. I'll find out more tomorrow." I shrugged, still smiling and he smiled back.

With Maddie not home, Brett took on the Frisbee play with Charlie while I cleaned up. Before we knew it, we were on our way to Melina's home.

Melina lived over in the direction of Pets and Paws, an older neighborhood with multiple signs announcing "Neighborhood Watch." I spotted people on the front porches of several of the small houses. We pulled up to Melina's and the person on the front porch next door, an older man, stood up and waved to us. Brett waved back and commented quietly, "I bet he doesn't miss a thing and will be over here to find out who we are as soon as we leave."

I nodded in agreement. Before I had a chance to respond, Maddie, Nedra, and a shepherd came running in our direction, all smiles. Melina and a man followed behind them. We made friends with "Shep" and Melina introduced her husband, Vincent. The girls chattered at us and eventually we managed to make our way home with promises of times for them to get together again.
.

CHAPTER 14

It was a nice day for a drive and Maddie agreed to tag along to Millicent College, not like she had a choice. She had her tablet and could email, read an ebook, or watch a movie while I was in the interview. At least she'd have a change of place. The winding road to Lynchburg was scenic. There were a few businesses along the road, a handful of bridges, and we spotted the river at some points.

With its multiple curves, a little snow or ice could make this a treacherous route to work. Today, though, the sun was shining and the car's AC was doing its job.

"I understand Alex got to go home yesterday. Yet, it's still not over, is it? Not for him or for me? The money and drug stuff – it's still out there, isn't it?"

I took a deep breath, surprised she was aware and unsure how to answer her. "You're right, Maddie. Until the police figure out where the money came from and how the envelopes got in your backpacks, the questions remain unanswered."

"And if the money and drugs are tied to that man's murder?"

"The same thing applies to the murder. Until they find out who killed Mr. Stories, they'll keep circling around to all the suspects and asking questions."

"You'll keep asking questions too, right?"

I nodded. "Probably. I like asking questions and figuring out puzzles."

She nodded back and turned on the radio. I followed the GPS directions and found a place to park with about 15 minutes to spare. Barely enough time to find some place for Maddie to hang out. Sure enough, there were benches, and tables, and vending machines in an alcove down the hall. A quick stop in the restroom to freshen up and I was off to meet Dr. Addison.

The interview with Dr. Addison and two other faculty was quick and nothing out of the ordinary. As expected, they requested I come back and teach a class. We discussed days, dates, and topics, and it was scheduled for later in the week. It had gone well.

I found Maddie where I'd left her, reading on her tablet. At almost 11 o'clock, it was a little too early for lunch. I spotted her bottle of water and a candy wrapper. She was all set. Me, I needed some caffeine, and not from a vending machine. "You ready to go?"

She smiled and nodded. "How'd it go? Did you get the job?" As she collected all her belongings, I explained there was a second step yet to go. A quick stop through the drive-through for my coffee and we were on our way home.

"What were you reading?"

"It's called *Turn It Up*. It's about a girls' singing group. It's funny. Nedra suggested it. I like it. What books…"

The next sound was metal on metal as a car hit us from behind, and then hit us again. I sped up while I requested the phone to call Brett and simultaneously told Maddie to call 9-1-1. The car hit us again and I was afraid to go much faster, remembering the curves up ahead. My call went to voicemail and I disconnected. Maddie had more luck.

"We're on the road back to Appomattox…" She pointed the phone at me.

"460 – we haven't gotten to the bridge yet."

"Someone keeps hitting our car. Sheridan's driving fast but they're driving faster."

"Yes, I'll stay on the line and put you on speaker."

"What kind of car?"

"The one hitting us is yellow. Looks like a jeep or one of those square boxy things. I can only see the front and it has a big black grate on it. We're in an Accord. Silver. We're approaching the bridge and I'm going to have to slow down. What should we do?"

"Slow down. Stop before the bridge. Keep your windows up and doors locked. Help is on the way."

"Okay. Maddie, you okay?"

She nodded, her eyes wide and teary. The car hit us again as I slowed down to the speed limit and they didn't. I strained to keep the car on the road and didn't relax even when I heard sirens.

"They're backing up, Sheridan. I'm scared."

"I know. I am too." I wanted to hold her, but in anticipation of being rammed I kept both hands on the steering wheel. To my relief, the sirens got louder and the car didn't come at us, but took to the off-road and disappeared. Obviously, the yellow monster had all-wheel drive. I pulled to the side of the road as far as I could and came to a stop. I reached for Maddie as I told the dispatcher our location.

"They left the road. We're stopped right before the bridge. I can see the flashing lights coming toward us."

"They see you. Stay safe." The voice on the phone disconnected. I pressed the phone button and directed "Call Brett" again. It rolled to voice mail. This time I left a message. "We've had some trouble but we're safe. Call when you can."

The police cruiser passed us, turned around and pulled in a distance behind us. He got out of his cruiser and talked to his shoulder. I got out my wallet, registration and insurance before he got to the window.

He signaled for me to open the window. "You two alright? Paramedics and fire are on the way." He took my papers as he spoke.

"I...I think so. Shook up for sure."

He handed me back my papers. "Are you able to drive the car?"

I wasn't exactly sure what he meant. "After the last hit, it felt like something was hitting the tires. I'm not sure it is drivable."

"Let me check." He walked to the rear of the car and got down to look underneath. I saw him talking again, but couldn't hear what he said.

"Ma'am, I need you and your daughter to get out of the car and go stand on the other side of the road, while we wait for the fire department. Please move now."

I grabbed my brief case and Maddie grabbed her backpack. We both climbed out my side and crossed the road.

"Walk a bit back down the road to where my car is, just in case."

We kept up with him as he walked down the road. I got my first look at the rear of my car. Maddie must have looked at the same time. We both gasped and she took my hand. I heard more sirens as the officer joined us.

"Ma'am, your car is not drivable. Do I have your permission to call a tow truck? There's only a couple options here and we prefer Travis Automotive, if that's okay." I nodded and he instructed someone to make the call. "Is there anyone we can contact for you or have you already called someone?"

"I tried to call my husband, but he isn't answering. He's with the State Police. Detective Brett McMann. Is there any way you can reach him?"

He smiled and stood a little straighter. "McMann's a good detective. I've attended a couple of lectures he gave. I'll see what dispatch can do." He turned and I only caught bits and pieces of what he said. The paramedics arrived from the other side of the bridge and the officer directed them to pull over just past us.

As they approached, the officer alerted them, "Fire is on the way. I didn't see any gasoline, but best to be safe. Take care of this side of the bridge. I'm going to the other side to stop any traffic."

The paramedics took our information and checked our vitals. We assured them we were not in immediate need of medical attention. The fire truck arrived and they conferred with the paramedics. I held onto Maddie as they investigated. Then the tow truck arrived and we discussed options for where to tow the car.

Not knowing anything about either shop he mentioned, I agreed with the driver's suggestion. We could always tow it again if need be. I snapped some pictures of the rear and sides before he hooked it up. He wasn't able to take us with him. The officer took our statements at the scene, but warned us he'd need to talk to us further at some later point. He volunteered to take us to the closest town. I took him up on the offer with hopes that by then Brett would contact us.

***

Where he dropped us off was more like a hamlet,

with a main street and about six buildings, including a small post office. The officer suggested we wait for Brett in the small local café. We both ordered the lunch special though I didn't taste much of it.

They boasted of the best ice cream in the county. Given the situation, I gave in to Maddie's request to try some. I wasn't sure about her, but I was starting to feel stiff and my head throbbed. I stared at my phone, willing Brett to call. The bell on the café's door sounded.

I looked up and there he was. He bounded the short distance and we both jumped into his arms. Maddie started crying while I did my best to hold back my tears. He soothed her and we all sat back down.

"You're both okay?"

"Uh huh. It was scary."

"More or less. Maddie was a trooper."

"Well, don't waste the rest of the ice cream. I can attest to this being the best ice cream." He smiled at Maddie and squeezed my hand. "Sure you're okay?"

"Stiffness is creeping in, headache. I took some ibuprofen. What are we going to do next?"

Maddie finished and we stood up. Brett paid the bill and we left.

"We're going to go home. And rest and recover. Call the insurance company. Then, I'm not sure. At some point, you'll need to review your statement. Sooner rather than later. Right now, they have alerted body shops across the state to be on the lookout – a BOLO – for a yellow all-wheel drive jeep-like model with black bars that shows signs of contact with a silver car."

We'd reached his car by then. "Okay."

I leaned back into the seat and closed my eyes. When I went to get out of the car, though, I was in pain. A trip to the emergency room, xrays, and a cervical collar added to the day's events.

CHAPTER 15

Several ibuprofen later and a night's sleep, I felt much better – at least as long as I didn't try to move too much without the cervical collar. Brett took the day off and we sat in the kitchen going over what happened while Maddie slept.

"You finished your interview and headed home, the same way you got there?"

"Same way, both ways. Not a lot of traffic, even in Lynchburg."

"Do you recall when you first saw the car that hit you?"

"We'd passed some business – maybe a factory. I didn't recognize the name. Until then, there'd been one or two cars behind us. I remember thinking we had the road to ourselves. Maddie was talking. I didn't see the car until it hit us the first time."

I started shaking and took a deep breath. "They hit us and we bounced forward. I kept going. I didn't want to stop with no other souls in sight. They backed up and hit us again or at least that was how it seemed. It may be they stopped and then came at us again. I tried speeding up, hoping to get to some place with more people. They sped up too. I called you and Maddie called 9-1-1. When I saw the sign for the bridge ahead, I knew we couldn't get on the bridge. Thankfully, the sirens coming toward us scared them off."

Brett's mouth opened and then closed. He spoke very carefully. "At any point, did you see the person or persons in the car?"

"Two. There were two people. I can't tell you much more than my impression they were both male. Maddie was watching from the side view mirror but I don't think she could see them once they were close enough to hit us."

"Think back to the ride to Lynchburg. Do you remember seeing the same car then? Yellow tends to stand out."

I shook my head. "Nope. Don't remember seeing any yellow cars on the way to Millicent. I remember a very old beat up truck and then the usual common gray tones and blacks."

He raked his fingers through his hair. "If you and Maddie were truly targets, how did they know where you were so they could wait for you to pass the factory?"

"You think it was coincidence? They were a couple of low lifes who decided hitting us was good fun? It sure felt personal."

"I agree. Too personal and too extreme. Still begs the question – who told them where you'd be and the car you'd be driving?"

I shrugged and winced. Obviously, shrugging was not a good idea.

Brett slapped his forehead. "I'm so sorry. I forgot to ask how the interview went. Did you get the job?"

I squeezed his hand. "Understood. Not yet. I have to go in tomorrow and teach a class I need to prepare for. Then they'll make a decision." Panic set in as I said it out loud.

"Okay. I hate to tell you this, but first you need to call your insurance agent." He tried to look serious but his eyes twinkled. "Then I'll keep Maddie occupied so you can work on your class."

My history with cars was not the best, through no fault of mine. I picked up my phone and got it over with, reporting where the car was so they could send an adjuster. It wasn't exactly new. Perhaps a new car was in my future as well as a new job. Brett set up the appointment for us to go over our statements after my class the next day. I showered and Maddie ate breakfast.

***

Brett and Maddie decided to go to the park with Charlie, while I worked on the class presentation and tried not to move too much. It was a summer class on introduction to psychology, and the topic was memory. I'd taught whole courses on learning and memory, so the content was familiar. The trick was deciding what would work best, allow for student interaction, and impress the other faculty who would be observing.

It didn't help that sitting up wasn't very comfortable. I pieced something together with the intent to go back and revise and review. Out of coffee, I ventured back to the kitchen as Maddie ran in from the garage, Charlie behind her.

"Sheridan, you won't believe it. Someone stole Karla's walker while she was in pool therapy. Nobody pays attention to who goes in or out of the pool there. When the therapist went to get the walker for her, it was gone. She was upset and had to stay in the pool until they found another walker. They still haven't found hers. Why would someone do that?"

My first thought of "to be mean" I kept to myself. "Do they have any idea who did it? Maybe someone thought it belonged to someone else?" I knew I was reaching, but …

Brett walked in, talking on the phone and not smiling. I looked to Maddie and mouthed "who's he talking to?"

"Mrs. Champlin. She asked to talk to him after Alex told me about the walker."

From the expression on his face, something else may have happened as well. "Why don't you get cleaned up? Lunch will be ready soon."

My phone rang, and I cringed as caller ID warned me it was my insurance agent. Short call. Car totaled and insurance cancelled. I also got the message I'd be looking for another agent. Now that I lived here, one in Appomattox would make sense, probably whomever Brett used.

Brett put his phone down and opened his arms. I didn't need any more invitation than that. He held me for a minute of two, his chin resting on my head. He moved back.

"Someone called the hospital where Angie worked and said they saw her poking around in the medication cabinet. Accused her of stealing drugs and selling them. Wouldn't leave their name. Police came and interviewed her, her co-workers, and they inventoried the medication cabinets she had a key for. All meds were accounted for, none were missing. No one there believes the accusation, but pending a full investigation, she will no longer have access to meds."

"Who made the call? That's slander or something isn't it?"

"Anonymous. Said they didn't want to get involved. They tried to trace the call, but it was one of those prepaid cell phones."

Maddie came into the kitchen with "Lunch?"

We laughed. Sometimes she wasn't hungry at all and sometimes she'd eat every hour. Looking at the pants and top, both stretched to the limit, I reminded myself we needed to go shopping.

"Oh, I heard from my friendly insurance agent and adjuster. The car is totaled, the check is on the way. I need to get back to Millicent College tomorrow and we need to go look at cars, and go shopping for Maddie."

Maddie grimaced. "I started to put all the clothes that don't fit good in a pile. I think the pile of what fits is smaller."

Brett glanced at her too tight top and bottoms. "Clothes shopping, then car shopping if you're up to it, but first some lunch."

My phone rang as I put sandwiches and macaroni salad on the table. It was Kim and I realized I'd never called her after the interview. I brought her up to date on everything while we ate.

Shopping for clothes was fun for Maddie, boring for Brett, and painful for me. Maddie ended up with shorts, capris, jeans and shirts. Me? A cervical collar in the summer heat and humidity should come with an ice pack built in or at least the "no sweat" material. Not to mention my hair got caught in the Velcro every time I tried to adjust it for comfort. Car shopping would have to wait.

CHAPTER 16

With no opportunity to shop around and decide on a new car, we decided to go with a rental for a week. The Hyundai Sonata didn't feel much different from my Accord and I loved the blue. All three of us were going to Lynchburg for me to teach the class. Brett wasn't taking any chances given someone tried to run us off the road. The ride was uneventful if not stressful as Maddie pointed out where we'd landed on the shoulder.

At Millicent, I left the cervical collar in the car, opting to grin and bear with the pain, rather than have to explain the injury. Maddie and Brett wandered toward the lounge area. The lesson went well. I got some laughs and saw the few faculty members who came nodding and making notes. Dr.

Addison walked me out to the hallway. He was smiling and promised he would be in touch before the weekend. He walked away and I walked down the hall to find Brett and Maddie.

Our next stop was the police station to sign off on our statements and answer any questions. On the way, Brett commented, "There were some students on a break I guess. They were not fans of Blake Buchanan."

"Huh? What did they say?"

"They called him a racist, Sheridan." Maddie chimed in before Brett had a chance.

"Oh, they did?"

"I don't think I ever want to meet him. They made him sound mean."

Brett nodded and mouthed "later" as we pulled into the small station. Not quite as country as Mayberry, but close. Inside we waited for the dispatcher to finish her phone call.

"Well, those two boys get away with everything. Their daddy and granddaddy take care of them." She nodded as if the person on the other end could see her.

"I agree with you. Caleb is the one who scares me. He's bigger and he doesn't say much. I bet he prefers to communicate with his fists."

The officer from the accident walked in and joined us as she continued. "I don't know why the Buchanan boys are hanging around here. Nothing but trouble."

The officer motioned for her to finish her call and

turned to us. "Officer Sparks, Detective. Nice to actually meet you, though I wish it were under better circumstances. I attended some of your lectures at the academy."

"I hope you enjoyed the lecture. I certainly appreciate your helping my wife and daughter out the other day. Any word on the BOLO?"

He nodded slightly. "Maybe. Maisy took a call a few minutes ago. Body shop the other side of Lynchburg called. Said a rental company brought in a yellow Highlander with some damage to the grill. It was stolen and when it was located, they noticed the damages. I came in to get the statements signed and ask a few follow up questions. When we finish up, I'll give him a call and then pay him a visit. I'll keep you posted if we find out anything."

"Good. Let's get this done."

Officer Sparks led the way and we walked over to a desk. He handed Maddie and me the statements he'd typed up from his notes. "Everything look right? Remember anything else?" We both shook our heads and we signed. Paperwork taken care of, we left.

***

The afternoon was quiet, though my heart raced each time my phone rang, hoping it was Dr. Addison. Melina called, then several telemarketers. Finally, the call I waited for came in.

"Dr. Hendley? Dr. Addison here."

"Yes, Dr. Addison."

"We'd like to offer you the Visiting Professor position for the coming year. No guarantees of anything beyond the one year. Is that agreeable?"

"Yes, that would be great. It would help to know what I'm teaching and my schedule of course. We discussed salary already."

"I'll get back to you with possible classes and schedule. I'll also send you the contract with benefits and salary for your review and signature. Please feel free to contact me if you have any questions."

"Thank you, Dr. Addison. I'll do that."

He cleared his throat. "Dr. Hendley? I happened to catch the news about the accident and something about your involvement in solving murders? I'm glad you weren't hurt. Let's try to keep the excitement level to a minimum next year, okay?"

I held it together as I agreed and disconnected. Then I laughed at his deadpan delivery as Brett walked in.

"What's so funny?"

I chortled. "I have a job! And then Dr. Addison mentioned my reputation in relation to murders. He must have been talking to Max."

He chuckled and gave me a kiss. "Congratulations. For the record, I'd prefer a few less murders on your plate, too."

"Anything new on this murder?"

"I talked to Chief Peabody. They've done due diligence with regard to the Champlin family. Apparently, someone – another anonymous tip – tried to pin it on Alex's father. Whoever it was obviously didn't realize he'd died. Being thorough, Peabody checked and there's no record that anyone in the Champlin family, including the father, ever bought a gun. The gun in the garbage can was not registered. Wiped clean like he suspected. That's no surprise."

"No resolution then. Anything tying Caleb and Luke to the murder or drugs?"

"No. Though it wouldn't be the first time Caleb was in trouble with law. He has a prior arrest for anger issues and assault. He got off with minimal community service. Mind you, he never did the service. He was such a problem at the community setting, they signed off just to get rid of him."

"No requirement for anger therapy?"

"It was mentioned and somehow got lost when the paperwork was done." His sneer told me he didn't believe that was an accident.

"What about Luke? He have a record too?"

"No record. But he has a reputation, much as we've already heard. Peabody hemmed and hawed. He wouldn't be surprised if either of them were dealing or using drugs. So far, no hard evidence though."

"What about Stories? Is it possible he was their source for drugs? Maybe the murder was some kind of drug deal gone bad?"

Brett shrugged. "From what Peabody shared, that's an option he's considering. Only Stories doesn't fraternize much with the Buchanans. Then there's his support of programs designed to prevent drug abuse or treat addictions."

"Could be on the up and up. Or all his efforts against drugs could be a ruse to cover up for his drug trade. Certainly, access to addicts would be good for business. From the autopsy, though there was no indication he was an addict. Nothing other than the envelopes of money to suggest he was involved at all."

I shook my head and winced. "Anything else?"

"Not really. Peabody thinks Caleb is good for it. He was acting off, nervous when the officers got to the scene. Blake Buchanan argued it was because he'd found his uncle murdered. Del Buchanan didn't say much in defense of his son. Interesting, though, someone made sure he had an attorney with him when he testified at Alex's hearing. The attorney probably rehearsed the testimony with Caleb in advance."

"And no word on who hit us? I thought the officer was checking on a lead?"

"He called. It might be the right car. Silver paint on the grill. It was stolen from the rental lot. They're checking for prints and they'll let us know if they can identify any of them."

Maddie bounded into the kitchen. "Can we go see Bella? I bet she's missing me. Pets and Paws is still open for another hour."

Brett glanced at me. "Do we need to go anywhere, do anything?"

"We need to look at cars. We also need to go grocery shopping. With all of us home, we are out of just about everything."

"Please, Daddy. We can stop at Pets and Paws on the way." She looked up at Brett and I almost laughed out loud.

He snorted. "Okay. A quick stop. Then the Honda dealership to at least window shop."

CHAPTER 17

It was a good thing Brett had accrued a lot of vacation and personal time. When Chief Peabody called and asked us to bring Maddie down to the station, I was glad he was available. Brett worked his jaw as he spoke with Peabody himself.

"They want to talk with both kids again." He shook his head. "We need to go as soon as Maddie eats and gets dressed. I can't imagine what they want to ask her and he wasn't very forthcoming."

"I'll finish getting breakfast ready. You may need to go wake her up. She's gotten used to sleeping late since she stopped going to camp."

He shuffled off and I could hear him trying to reassure her. Judging from her tear-filled eyes and her shaking hands, he wasn't very successful.

"Am I going to be arrested and put in jail, like Alex was?"

"They only want to ask you some questions. We'll

be right there with you. We know you didn't have anything to do with money or drugs." He took her into his arms and I saw his concern in his eyes and the set of his chin.

We picked at breakfast, and then I helped Maddie pick out her clothes. The short ride seemed to take forever. Maddie gasped as we exited the car and she saw Alex, his mother, and sister enter the station. At Peabody's request, only Brett accompanied Maddie into the office. When Angie accompanied Alex, Karla and I kept each other company. Eric Pinsky joined us about the same time Alex and Angie came out.

"Sorry it took so long. I got here as quickly as I could."

Angie nodded. "I appreciate it. We wanted to get it over with. At least find out what they wanted."

Brett and Maddie joined us as she finished. "How about we take this party some where else? Al's? Whoever gets there first, grab a booth?"

***

Not quite time for the lunch rush, too late for breakfast for a weekday, Al's wasn't crowded. We got a booth big enough for six and Eric pulled up a chair at the end. Once the waitress took our orders, Eric looked around the table. "Well?" Brett motioned to Angie and Alex to go first.

"The questions were all about Luke and Caleb Buchanan?" Angie turned to Alex.

He continued, "They asked me if they dealt drugs. I told them I didn't know. Then something about an anonymous tip and did I have anything to do with that. It was weird."

Brett tilted his head as Maddie jumped in. "Same with me. Asked if they were into drugs. How should I know? Maybe they heard the rumors?"

Eric commented, "Very…odd."

Brett shrugged but his expression was pensive. "No clue."

"I was very worried. My neighbors mentioned someone had been by to ask questions. Mrs. Daniels in particular. She was insulted they thought she was lying about being at our house when that man was murdered. I thought… I didn't expect them to ask about those Buchanan boys."

Sodas and coffees arrived. Brett opened his mouth to speak, but Eric beat him to the punch. "Were these police talking to your neighbors?"

"Mrs. Daniels said two men came to her house. Said they were investigating and wanted to ask her questions. She didn't say they were police." Angie glanced from Eric to Brett and back to Eric. "Were they police?"

"Don't worry about it Angie. I'll stop by and talk to Mrs. Daniels myself. Not everyone who asks questions is the police though. Always ask for identification if someone doesn't volunteer it."

Brett nodded and she seemed to relax. To shift the conversation, I asked, "Any plans for the afternoon?"

Angie explained, head down, "I had to switch my work schedule a bit, so I'm going into work. Mrs. Daniels will keep her eyes on Alex and Karla." She turned to Maddie. "What about you?"

"We didn't decide yet. Can we take Charlie to Pets and Paws to meet Bella? Mrs. Chantilly said it would be okay now. Please?"

We all laughed and Brett caved. "If it's okay with Sheridan. We'll have to postpone car shopping if we do."

I agreed, not in any rush to decide on a car. We stopped at home to get Charlie then headed over to Pets and Paws.

Charlie was beside herself when we entered Pets and Paws. She'd start to go in one direction, spot another dog, and change directions. We guided her in the direction of the mama and pups. Brown Sugar lifted her head and watched Charlie as we walked in. Susie was there and helped her stand and we introduced Charlie to Brown Sugar first. I hadn't realized how thin she was before. The introduction went well and Charlie lay down. Brown Sugar did as well. Some of the pups searched out mama and others checked out Charlie.

Brett and I moved out of the way and Mrs Chantilly joined us as she bustled here and there passing out her biscuits. "Poetic justice don't you think? I heard police got an anonymous tip about a drug deal going down and caught Luke and Caleb with the goods. Be sure Maddie understands that pup's not ready to leave yet."

"Excuse me?"

"Yup, late last night. No one showed up to buy the drugs though. Blake Buchanan is yelling 'set up' and 'entrapment' only dispatch has the call logged. Oh, look. Charlie's playing with the pups. Mama is watching, but seems okay. More dogs coming later today."

She turned and walked away, Brett and I still stunned.

"How…?" Brett put his finger to his lips to silence me as Maddie came running.

"Charlie likes Bella best, too. I'm sure she does."

Brett rolled his eyes and I chuckled. It was a draw on who it was harder to get to leave Pets and Paws, Charlie or Maddie. We stopped at the Honda dealership and talked to the sales person to see what they could give us for cost and financing. Maddie was bored, but hung in there long enough to stop at the Hyundai dealer. For her part, Charlie hammed it up and enjoyed all the attention at both dealerships.

In the midst of our discussion of Honda or Hyundai, Chief Peabody called. Prints in the Highlander were a match for Caleb and Luke. He was following up on it.

It was after dinner when Brett got a call and took it outside. Usually, that meant it was work related. In this case, it was Peabody again.

"He thanked us for coming in so quickly. He apologized for any inconvenience and explained about the anonymous tip and drug bust last night. I got the feeling he hoped Maddie or Alex knew something or someone who bought drugs from them."

"Did he mention the entrapment explanation?"

"No. Apparently they were able to get search warrants and not only found more drugs at Caleb's house, but also more cash, in envelopes. Either $200 or $250 in each, like the ones in the kid's backpacks and with Stories. He wanted to let us know, with what they discovered, we didn't need to worry any longer."

"I sure hope that's the case. Do they think Caleb killed Stories, then?"

"That one is still up in the air. No way to connect him or Luke to the murder. Now, he's trying to get them on crashing into you. Blake Buchanan hired a good attorney and nobody's talking."

Before turning in, I diagrammed all the people involved from Alex and Maddie to Luke, Caleb, and Stories. The only common denominator was the money envelopes.

CHAPTER 18

The phone ringing woke me up. Seeing Kim's name worried me and I sat up, expecting the worst.

"What's up?"

"You sound groggy. Were you still asleep?"

"Yes. Why aren't you? It's not even 8 o'clock yet."

"I know. I set the alarm to get up to call you. Do you guys have plans today?" She sounded like she was in a good mood and excited about something. I wondered…

"No. Why?"

"Marty and I were out last night and heard some people talking about a Lawrence Stories who'd been murdered."

"What?" My loud response disturbed Brett's

sleep. He stirred and opened his eyes. I put the phone on speaker.

"See, I knew I'd get your attention. There's some kind of informal Civil War re-enactment near North Shore today. Apparently, there's a group of closet historians and Civil War buffs in the area. Trust Marty to be in touch with them. Every year they get together and re-enact some battle. Like a war game."

"Was there a battle fought near North Shore?"

"No, though apparently there were a number of battles fought in Virginia, more than I knew. They pick a battle and a place. The man who was answering all our questions, Linc Grantly, explained they want to have a little fun and an excuse to get together and talk about the war and history. He said there are too many people at the bigger, official re-enactments like at Gettysburg."

"Interesting. I wonder if they do one here? Of course, this is where Lee surrendered, so perhaps not. What did they say about Stories?"

"Stories was one of the closet historians. Funny you mentioned Lee's surrender. They originally planned a different battle, but in Stories' honor, they are going to re-enact that battle complete with Lee's surrender. Linc explained Stories was very active in their group, albeit with loyalties on the Union side."

Hearing Marty's voice explained a little how Kim was awake and talking so early, and about history no less. "Hi Marty. So are you a Civil War enthusiast too?"

"It is a very interesting part of history. I've never been to a re-enactment, so it has some appeal for a unique way to spend a Saturday. We wondered if you and Brett and Maddie wanted to join us. Maybe learn something about Stories at the same time."

Brett had been listening for most of the conversation. "Let us check with Maddie and see if we can sell her on the idea. What time does this thing start?"

"Hey, Brett. They have a meet and greet beginning about 9 o'clock. Linc said there's coffee and pastry and lots of milling around. Then the soldiers get in their costumes and the park is turned into the site of the battle. The speech honoring Stories is set for 11 o'clock right before the action. The battle is fairly short and then everyone has lunch."

"Any bloodshed with diverging opinions? I've had enough excitement this week with Whistklan."

"Geesh, nothing like that. Not from what he said at least. In fact, no one gets to choose which side they're on. They draw a card, either blue or gray with their role, and that's the army they serve in for the day. And they don't draw the card until they register on site."

"Interesting. Hopefully, we can convince Maddie."

The timing didn't leave us with room to spare and I jumped out of bed and headed for the kitchen as soon as the call disconnected. Definitely needed some caffeine. It was the morning of surprises and Maddie wandered in while I was still drinking my first cup.

"Nedra called and invited me to go to her house and hang out, go swimming, and stuff. Can I go? Please?"

Brett walked in and I caught his eye. "Let me check with Melina on times and be sure she's okay with it. Unless you'd rather come to a Civil War re-enactment with your dad and me?"

She grimaced and then caught herself. "I think I'd rather spend time with Nedra if that's okay."

Brett nodded and I called Melina. I explained we'd be back late afternoon and she was fine with it.

***

Breakfast and showers done, we dropped off Maddie and headed to meet Kim and Marty in North Shore. I'd printed out directions and inputted the information for Waze to direct us. I was not sure how to get there from Appomattox, and my sense of direction was pitiful. It was a pleasant drive and we soon saw signs directing us to the park. My neck was feeling better and when we got there, I left the collar in the car.

We made our way toward the event site. People milled around, friendly – most obviously knew each other. Not a large crowd. I'd checked online about what to expect, and this was definitely on a smaller scale than other re-enactments with only about 40-50 participants. They were easily identified by the gray or blue card hanging around their neck, with a few already in uniform. There were about as many spectators, all engaged in conversation. To my surprise, not everyone was southern white. There was a smattering of African Americans, Asians, and Hispanics. From the snippets I heard, the common thread was their interest in the Civil War. We smiled as we walked toward the coffee and snacks to find Kim and Marty.

I spotted a poster of Stories and his family. It was the first time I'd seen a picture of him or Lila. He was a handsome man with light brown hair, what some might call mousy brown, and brown eyes. His nose looked like it had been broken at some point in time, I imagined fighting for his causes. He was smiling, eyes hooded, his attention on Lila, not the camera.

Lila was striking with chiseled features, and milky white skin, blue eyes and long strawberry blonde hair. She wore a simple sheath of pale green that hugged her curves.

One of the boys was in uniform. I realized this picture must have been when he entered the service or graduated boot camp. All three boys had their father's brown eyes. Two had his light brown hair; the shortest had strawberry blonde hair and favored his mother more than the other two. It made sense they would be here given Stories was being honored.

We continued to walk and I spotted one of the sons ahead of us. "Brett, he looks like the middle son."

We continued to walk in the same direction and the son veered toward a trash can. Brett held my arm and we stopped. Brett turned as if to kiss me as the young man gave a furtive glance around. Then he reached into a pocket and dropped something into the trash. With another quick glance, he took off at a much brisker pace.

"Definitely the middle boy from the poster." Suspicious, Brett made for the trash can to check it out.

"Do you have a napkin or something I can use?"

I handed him the napkin from around my cup. He pulled out what looked like a cell phone. Brett looked around and then pulled out his cell and punched in a number.

"Chief Peabody? Brett McMann here. Do you still have the number for the phone that called in your last anonymous tip? Or any of them?"

"You do? Someone threw a cell phone away where I am. May be nothing, or not related to the case at all, but can you call that number?"

Immediately, the phone he'd retrieved from the trash sounded the standard ring tone.

"Hear that? I have the phone and I know who dumped it. I just need to get a name for you. We're in North Shore right now and so is the phone and person."

Brett nodded as he listened to the Chief's reply. "We'll be back in Appomattox by 4 o'clock, if not sooner. We can bring the phone and make a statement when we get back to town." He looked around as he put his phone away. "I don't suppose you have a plastic bag or something in your purse?"

I shook my head. "Lots of stuff, but no baggies. Can you wrap it up with more napkins? Put it in the zipper section in my purse?"

"Zipper. Hard to tell if there will be any usable prints, but at least we can try to not wipe the phone clean."

Handing him my almost empty coffee cup, I emptied the makeup and stuff out of the zippered section, letting it all fall to the bottom of the purse. He gingerly set the phone in and I zipped it closed.

"Okay, let's go find Marty and Kim, see what else we can unearth." I took a last gulp of coffee and tossed the cup. Anyone who saw us would think that was why we stopped at the trash can.

He took my hand and we wandered some more.

"Sheridan, over here." Marty's voice pinpointed where they were. We joined them with hugs all around.

"You're walking around without a cup of coffee? We need to fix that. And wait until you try the cheese pastries. So good." Kim linked her arm with mine and started walking. She turned around only long enough to add, "Come on you guys, we need to get some food and seats before 11 o'clock.".

CHAPTER 19

Not intended for a stage, chairs were arranged in double rows to form a rectangle in the most open part of the park. The ground wasn't flat and I wondered which side got the advantage of not having to fight uphill. Men in faded uniforms of gray and blue gathered in the middle, carrying old style rifles. I recalled reading about a re-enactment where someone substituted real bullets with dire results. I shuddered at the thought. Kim tapped my arm.

"There's a woman in Union blue. For sure not authentic to the Union army."

I nodded as Marty chimed in. "And the African American man fighting for the Confederacy has to create some internal conflict for a few of these folks."

As I looked around, I spotted the tattered Confederate flag and a similar vintage Union flag. One man in gray and one in blue wheeled an antique looking cannon onto the field. I couldn't spot the higher in command in blue. In gray, a man sported a beard and had a vague resemblance to pictures I remembered of General Lee. Musing about the motivation of the participants on the field was cut short by a trumpet blare.

"Welcome to our annual civil war re-enactment. I'm Lincoln Grantly, the leader of the Civil War Enthusiast Club here in North Shore. As I'm sure most of you know, one of Virginia's biggest enthusiasts, Lawrence Stories, died recently. I'd like to introduce his wife, Lila, and their three sons, Ryan, Joshua, and Tyler, who are here with us today. Before we begin, I'd ask all to bow your heads for a moment of silence for Stories."

As their names were called, they nodded. Ryan wore his dress blues, while his brothers wore jeans and sport shirts. Clearly, it was Joshua who dumped the phone. The park was amazingly quiet for the minute.

"I'm still having difficulty realizing our friend and fellow enthusiast will not again be with us. As a man, he was a champion of those not always championed – minorities, women, the disabled. He was most known – and probably disliked – for his outspoken rhetoric against the confederacy and NRA. Best time we had was when he pulled a gray card. He manned up and played the role he was dealt. Today, in his honor, we will re-enact the battle when Lee surrenders, not for the accuracy but the outcome of the battle. We're pretty sure Stories would appreciate it. Places everyone."

I'd never been to a reenactment. The participants ran to their positions and then plowed forward in mass. Lots of rifle fire, smoke, and people falling down. And then it was over, more Union soldiers still standing and impinging on the Confederate line. Behind me, a man critiqued the re-enactment from the number of soldiers to the distance between the armies and the time it took before Lee surrendered. Obviously, it fell short of his expectations, but others clapped and cheered as the players all stood up and took a bow.

Linc took the microphone. "I hope you enjoyed the show, though somewhat shortened due to the sudden change in the battle chosen. While we are all Civil War enthusiasts, we cannot forget the downside to this or any war. Families are torn apart and young soldiers lose their lives, or worse, their ability to move past the war. As with every occasion, I'll ask for a minute of silence as we remember the lives lost in this battle and all battles, on all sides."

Again, the park became silent. After a pause, he ended with, "We'll give these folks a chance to clean up and lunch will be served shortly."

Everyone talked at once and the noise level rose. I noticed the Stories family had disappeared at some point in the festivities. The four of us walked a distance from the crowd.

"Interesting, huh? What did you think, Sheridan?"

"Interesting for sure, Marty." Reflecting on the side bits of conversation I'd heard, I added, "I never knew there were this many people interested in discussing theories as to why Lee's strategies didn't work and how he lost the war."

"Me neither." Kim agreed.

"I'm actually more surprised though how well those who favor the confederacy so easily socialize with those who oppose them and vice versa."

Marty shook his head. "For these folks, most of them anyway, this is an intellectual exercise, not an emotional one. These are mostly historians, with a few romanticists still enthralled with 'Gone with the Wind' and the hype of the southern plantation. This is about history, not politics."

"History aside, I'm all for the present and future. Let's grab some lunch. Then Brett and I need to get back."

***

Brett called Peabody from the car. He described what we'd observed and identified Joshua as the one who dumped the phone in the trash. Back in town, our first stop was the police station to turn in the phone. We watched as Joshua and Lila were ushered into the station. Peabody took them into his office, but left the door partly open.

"Now, Joshua, we received a report from a reliable source you dumped a prepaid cell phone into the trash today. Funny thing, the anonymous tip we got about your cousins came from that phone. Can you explain it to me?"

"My dad knew they were dealing drugs. I heard him trying to get them to quit, offering to get them help if they had a habit. He threatened to turn them in if they didn't get straight. I heard what they said after my dad was killed – he had envelopes of money, drug money when he was killed. Luke and Caleb. They must've planted those on his body after they killed him. They're always above the law. Someone had to get their drug business out in the open."

His voice got louder as he spoke and I thought I heard Lila gasp.

"Now calm down, son. What did you do?"

"I didn't do anything illegal. I called Caleb's number from the sheet of family phone numbers using the prepaid cell phone. Told him my name was Jonas Blackwell and I needed a score, didn't care how much it cost. He gave me what I can only guess was a high price. I acted desperate, said I needed it ASAP. He agreed to the time and place. All I had to do was make an anonymous tip and wait. The police can't do that. I can. I did. Then I dumped the phone in North Shore. How'd it end up here?"

"Someone saw you drop the phone, Joshua. Wondered why you'd ditch the phone. You sound like you knew Caleb was involved in drugs. What can you tell me?"

"I never hung out with him or Luke. Well, or any of the cousins much. Not Mark or Michael either. They all seemed pretty close though and with the word around school they were into drugs… Mom and Dad discouraged it."

"What did you hear, Joshua? It might help us figure out who killed your dad."

"Mostly, just to stay away from them. Caleb's a

little on the odd side and Luke has a love 'em and leave 'em rep. They're bullies and they make up stories about anyone who slights them. Once last year, Caleb made a snide comment about my parents. Ryan stopped me from letting him have it. I kept my distance and made sure Tyler did too."

"Okay. Thank you both for coming in."

As we heard chairs scraping the floor, we moved over to the other side of the room and waited for them to leave. Once they were out the door, Peabody waved us in, shaking his head.

"Nice catch, McMann. At least we have confirmed who made this tip and can prove it wasn't police entrapment. Not going to go down well with the Buchanans that it was one of their own."

"What's the status on Caleb and Luke now?"

"Both home, under parental control." He snorted. "Judge is third or fourth cousin I think. Anyone else, they'd be my guests. Blake Buchanan? I heard he's gathered his sons together for a meeting. He told Brandon he was going to get to the bottom of this. I hope he's not too upset by what he finds. It's not smelling too pretty from my perspective."

"Where's that leave Maddie and Alex?"

Peabody smiled. "Pretty sure we all agree they were set up. Checked with all Alex's teachers from last year. No problems, everything glowing, a good kid, responsible, model citizen. No indication he ever used. No unexplained money to suggest he dealt. Just these envelopes that keep showing up. My guess is either Caleb and Luke made up the money from their own coffers or their supplier is wondering where the money is."

He stood and we followed suit. At least part of the mystery was resolved.

CHAPTER 20

On the way home, we stopped at Seafood Grill & Deli for take out. Brett took a call and stayed in the car, while Maddie and I went in to get the food. She was chattering away about the great time she had with Nedra and suddenly stopped. She grabbed my arm and stiffened as a tall young man approached us. He was in jeans and a t-shirt, slim with muscles evident through the thin material. He reminded me of the posters of California surfers with white blonde hair, blue eyes, tan, and a swagger.

"Hi Maddie. Missed you at camps." He leered first at her and then at me. "Nice."

Ignoring him as best I could, I tsked. "Maddie, I forgot what your dad wanted. Can you go ask him please?" As she ran for the door, I added, "Thanks!"

I turned my back on him and pretended to study the menu, feeling his eyes on me the whole time. He moved next to me and leaned in, invading my personal space.

"That wasn't real nice of her. She never introduced us. I'm Luke Buchanan."

"Nice to meet you." I tried to catch the waitress' attention and moved my body away from him. "Sally, when you get a chance?" She nodded toward the back of the deli where a group of men were engaged in conversation.

"Yeah, Sally, we need some ice tea back there. My grandfather sent me to tell you." He shifted his attention back to me. "You must be new around here."

Brett made his appearance in time to hear his comment and bristled. "She is new around here. Moved here when we got married. I don't think we've met. Brett McMann."

Luke cringed, recovering quickly and with attitude. "Ah! You must be Maddie's dad then. Best lock her up. She's hot." He snickered and I squeezed Brett's arm. Next thing I knew, another man grabbed Luke's shoulder.

"What's wrong with you, Luke? You don't want to be talking with the detective here without an attorney present. Did you tell Sally about the tea?"

Luke nodded and his sneer disappeared. The tension rolled off Brett as I studied the slightly more portly and older version of Luke. He reminded me of the man at the courthouse and then at Pets and Paws. He didn't take his hand off Luke's shoulder as he propelled him in the direction of the table.

I leaned into Brett and whispered, "Breathe. Just breathe." I was about to suggest pizza instead and Sally was there with "The usual? Seafood pasta salad, shrimp, coleslaw, the works?"

I nodded and she disappeared. A few minutes later, she handed us a big bag and checked us out.

***

Curiosity was killing me, yet I knew Brett wouldn't want to talk in front of Maddie. She never said anything about the run-in with Luke and neither did we. She relaxed once we left the Deli and ate. During dinner though, she looked like she was ready to nod off. She helped clean up and then headed for her room to watch a movie. My bet was she'd be asleep before the movie got interesting.

"Wine?"

"That sounds good. Need to wind down. It's been a long day."

I pulled the bottle out of the refrigerator and grabbed two glasses. We stayed in the kitchen so our voices would be less likely to carry to Maddie's room.

"You going to tell me who he was?"

"Shane Buchanan. Remember I told you about him. Peabody said Blake Buchanan called a family meeting. I didn't think they'd have him come all the way down. How could he be involved?"

I shrugged. "Strength in numbers? There was a big group of them. I recognized Caleb, I think. He's a lot huskier than most of the others, so he stands out. One man was definitely older, more stately. Blake Buchanan?"

"He was there, yes. And he was the oldest one, the patriarch and picture of the prototypical southern gentleman."

"If Shane was the one that came up to Luke when you showed up, I think I saw him at lunch the other day when we ran into to Angie and Karla, the courthouse this morning and then outside Pets and Paws."

"You sure you saw Shane?"

"Not sure, but someone who looked like him. The other two must be the other two sons?"

"I've never met Delaney or Brandon, so I can't say for sure. That would be my guess. They all look alike. Other than Luke and Caleb, there were two other younger ones. Likely Michael and Mark, their younger brothers."

"Did Shane have any children?"

"Yes, and not surprisingly, both boys. About the same age as Joshua and Tyler Stories if I remember correctly."

"Do you think Blake Buchanan is behind the drugs and murder? A family affair?"

"Blake and I may not agree on political views, from the confederacy to current politics… If he's involved in anything illegal, he's hid it well. He may be pompous and a bit racist, but within the law. Shane, I wouldn't be so sure of. Luke? He's pushing the edge or over it." He shook his head and clenched his fists.

"Shane seemed to have a sobering effect on him. He lost a bit of his bluster. And he now knows you're a detective."

"Not sure if that's good or bad. What I caught walking in? His attitude? He might view my being a detective as a challenge." He exhaled. "Is Maddie too young for self-defense classes? I'd rather that than teaching her to shoot."

"Amen. Do you think Luke killed Stories? What about Caleb? Why would either – or both of them – be meeting with Stories at the historical park? Was it connected to his views on the confederacy? Irony to be killed where Lee surrendered?"

"That seems like a stretch, Sher. I'd go with the obvious. It's a big park. Lots of people walking in and out. From the map, there are multiple trails and cabins. Easy to find some place for a quiet meet. Or murder."

"It's possible he met with Caleb and Luke to talk to them about the drug thing and threatened to turn them in, and it soured from there. Maybe even an accident."

"The gun. It wasn't one of theirs, not registered anyway. I have no doubt they had easy access to pistols and rifles. No, this was a throw-away gun. One nobody would miss or care if it went missing. That would mean not an accident. Premeditated. Planned."

Brett's phone rang. "Uh huh." "Good news." "Definitely." "Thanks for calling."

He hung up and let out a deep breath. "Peabody.

Caleb admitted to planting the money in Alex and Maddie's backpacks. Said it was Luke's idea to steal the pizza money and then blame Alex and Maddie. The only opportunity they had to stash the money in their backpacks was before they snatched the money. So they guessed how much – obviously they guessed too high. Then added more to make it interesting."

"But why?"

"Luke was mad Maddie rejected him. And Alex because he was getting in the way of his attempts to win Maddie over. Luke admitted to calling in the tip about Alex and the pizza money. Alex and Maddie are officially cleared now."

We clinked our glasses.

"What about the Highlander and crashing into Maddie and me?"

"The story being put out by their attorney is they stopped at the rental place and rented the car. They took it for a drive and weren't impressed, so they returned it. That's how their prints got on it. Peabody's trying to check the story with the rental agency, see if there's a record of them renting the car. Only it will take time."

"Why can't they show them pictures of all of the Buchanans and ask if they recognize any of them?"

He put his hands up. "If they had some indication of who it might be, they'd do a line up. The problem, in case you didn't notice, is the strong family resemblance among the brothers, and even the cousins. Only Caleb stands out."

CHAPTER 21

It started out as a lazy Sunday morning. Even Brett and I slept in later than usual. Maddie lumbered into the kitchen, her phone in hand.

"Let me check and call you back." She disconnected and reached for the orange juice.

"Do you want pancakes?" I asked.

She nodded and I passed the plate and syrup. Brett cleared his throat and we waited. I took a wild guess at what she needed to "check" and asked, "Any plans for today?"

Brett tried not to laugh and coughed instead. "No, I don't have any. We do still need to decide on a car and get insurance taken care of, probably do some grocery shopping, start back to school shopping..."

"Wait! Can we go to Pets and Paws? Nedra's

going with her mom. We could take Charlie again so she can bond with Bella." Charlie jumped up from her bed and put her head in Maddie's lap, tail wagging.

"Well, we do have to…"

"But don't you see? I'll stay at Pets and Paws with Charlie while you run your errands."

Brett sagged into his chair as she pleaded. "Okay. Your room better be clean though and you'll help with the laundry later, right?"

She nodded and shoveled in another mouthful of pancakes before bolting with her phone.

"Sher, I think I'm in trouble here." He shook his head, smiling as he gazed down the hall.

I chuckled. "You did good. Added a few chores in there. Hopefully, it's not too busy at Pets and Paws and nobody tries to adopt Charlie."

Not too much later, we pulled into Pets and Paws. Charlie led the way up the steps and into the door. Mrs. Chantilly clapped her hands when she saw us.

"How wonderful to see you all. That includes you, Charlie." She leaned over and petted Charlie. "It's not your day to volunteer, Sheridan. What brings you here on a Sunday?" Her eyes twinkled as she directed her question to Maddie.

"Charlie needs to bond with Bella, and I'll help make sure Bella gets enough to eat. And … and I can help with the other mama and pups, too. Nedra's gonna help."

After some affection from Mrs. Chantilly, Charlie let Maddie lead her to the side room and Bella. Mrs.

Chantilly watched them go. "Oh, to be so young again. We have another new mama in there. Not quite sure what she is and her pups, well now that's a motley crew. Can you believe it?"

I was with her until the end. Confused, I asked, "Believe what?"

"Well, the strings Blake Buchanan pulled. First, he gets those boys released because their parents are responsible. Responsible my foot. Rich, is more like it. You know the vet cleared Bella, right? As long as you monitor her weight and she continues to grow, she's good to go." She nodded vigorously. A couple with a little girl walked in.

"Good afternoon. I'm Mrs. Chantilly. Did you have a type of dog or size in mind today?"

The woman said, "Something small, I think." At the same time, the man said, "A big one, for protection." The little girl muttered "Doggie" and pointed as Charlie bounded over to me.

I picked her up and held her, hopefully sending a message. Mrs. Chantilly took the middle road. "Is that about the size you're thinking of? Not too big, not too small. Like the three bears."

I almost laughed out loud. Instead, I approached the little girl. "This is my dog, Charlie. Would you like to pet her? She's very friendly."

The little girl giggled and petted her while Mrs. Chantilly flitted around. "How about if you take them to the back. Some are bigger, but not all of them. Chloe is a sweetie."

"Great idea, Sheridan. Come along, let's go meet

Chloe." She sashayed off with the family following her. Brett and I stepped into the other room and watched Maddie with the mama and her pups. I counted and there was one missing, hopefully adopted out. I put Charlie down and she walked over to the group.

I heard a growl behind me. She looked to be a Shepard mix and her pups. I reassured the mama and placed Charlie's leash on Maddie's wrist. "You need to keep a hold of her. The mama over there is protective and worried about her pups." Nodding toward Charlie curled up on the other side of her, I added, "And Charlie's spooked by her growl."

Maddie nodded and then jumped up, startling all of us, puppies, and the mamas. "Nedra! Come see."

I moved out of the way and Melina took a stance between the two dogs and their pups. "Sometimes, Mrs. Chantilly… it would be safer if they were in crates and not loose like this."

Brett nodded agreement. He spotted an empty large crate against the wall and placed it between the two dogs and their pups. Not quite the same, but now there was a barrier and the Shepard stopped growling.

We were about to leave Maddie and Nedra in Melina's capable hands when Mrs. Chantilly planted herself between us and the door.

"It's too much. Blake Buchanan arranged for Caleb to be admitted to drug rehab. The drugs made him do it, he said."

Before I could stop myself, I asked, "Do what? What did he do?"

"Dealing drugs. He's arguing Caleb dealt drugs to support his own habit. Led into temptation by his cousin. I'm tempted myself sometimes. And to beat all? Luke is the innocent here. They found roofies in Luke's possession along with other drugs, but he's the golden boy. What I wouldn't do for the chance to tell off Shane Buchanan. You had a run in with him, didn't you, Detective."

Brett's mouth dropped and I decided to take advantage of her jumping topics. Waving toward the side room, I asked, "When did the Shepard mix in there deliver? She's a bit protective."

"Not sure. Yup, you're right, some Shepard for sure. She was brought in with the pups. Probably right after, but no telling. Might be a good idea…"

She tilted her head and pointed toward the cage between the dogs. "That was the good idea, but I don't recall … anyway, I suspect she'll be okay in a couple days. Those boys, now, I'm not so sure about them."

"Maddie's going to stay here for a while with Nedra and Melina. We need to look at cars and then we'll be back. Hopefully, she and Charlie won't be a bother."

"No bother, dear. Caleb was driving the car that hit you, you know. Those boys, they do like those all-wheel drive cars." She didn't skip a beat as the family came toward us. "So what did you think of Chloe?"

"She licked me."

The father smiled but it didn't reach his eyes. "We're not sure. We'll give it some thought." He hurried his wife and daughter out the door.

Mrs. Chantilly smiled, "Biscuits. I need more biscuits." She didn't say anything else. She turned and disappeared in the direction of the kitchen.

I yelled, "Later" and we left.

In the car, I asked Brett, "What do you think of Mrs. Chantilly?"

He laughed. "She is something, isn't she? A bit eccentric. I've interacted more with her since you started volunteering here. One of the other Detectives, James Zabry, he worked most of the cases closer to here. He'd muse about her sometimes. She seems to have details of what's going on with the locals that's kind of hard to imagine."

"You mean like what she said about Blake and Caleb? How would she know all the details if it's not public knowledge yet? Her daughter Lacie?"

"Not Lacie. She wouldn't have some of the information Mrs. Chantilly seems to have access to. I forget what it was about. Zabry proffered she either bugged the police station or had ESP. Some case he was on. She seemed to have facts well before anyone else."

"Makes you wonder who she's talking to and where her loyalties are. She sure isn't a fan of Luke or Caleb. Or Shane for that matter."

He nodded. "Ask Melina. Maybe she's got a handle on her. She's been here a long time. Even Angie might know her story. She's harmless I'm sure."

CHAPTER 22

With Luke and Caleb supposedly not available for camp, Brett agreed, reluctantly, for Maddie to go back to camp. While I waited for the actual contract and paperwork, I searched the Millicent website for important dates. With no clue what I would be teaching, it was difficult to prepare. I did need to figure out where Brett stuck my Cold Creek boxes. Searching in the garage, I found them, only couldn't get to them easily. Brett would have to rearrange again and grant me access.

In the meantime, the priorities were on contacting Brett's insurance agent and arranging insurance for the Hyundai. The hassle would be the name thing. Brett and I had discussed it before we got married, and at least for now, I hadn't changed my name. My psychologist license and the list of other forms and agencies was too overwhelming. We agreed not to make a big deal of it and I answered to Mrs. McMann as easily as Dr. Hendley. Paperwork was where it got sticky.

Insurance arranged, I called Melina to see if she was available to go to lunch. She agreed. We met up at the Seafood Grill and Deli, one of the few times I ate in the restaurant instead of take out.

"So how's it going? Maddie back in camp today?"

"Yes. And she hasn't called so I guess everything is going well. And Nedra?"

"She's hanging out at home. Supposed to be cleaning her room. I'm sure you know how that goes."

I chuckled. "I'm learning. It certainly has been an interesting couple of weeks. And to think I was complaining of boredom. Is this typical Appomattox county?"

She shook her head. "Not hardly. Last time there was a scandal was several years ago. Lots of rumors with Blake Buchanan in the middle of it all. No murder though."

"Melina, how long have you known Mrs. Chantilly?"

She laughed. "Almost since she first showed up here. Several of us helped her clean out the ground floor. It was something else. She's what my mama would call an 'odd duck.' She runs the shelter, she manages to do ordering, track adoptions, keep up with the vet and care of the dogs, all of them. I've never seen her turn away a dog, unless it was contagious. Even then she took the dog to the vet herself."

"That's 'odd' because?"

"I've seen the confused expression on your face, Sheridan. She'll be talking about one thing and all of a sudden she comes out with something not at all connected. Sometimes I'm not sure she even sees the relevance. It's like it comes out of her mouth, she hears it, and realizes she let something slip. Immediately goes back to the original topic."

"I did notice the breaks in topics. She sure seems to get information quick. Any idea how she finds out all the stuff, like about Caleb and Luke? Maybe from Lacie?"

"Lacie doesn't have much to do with her. She adopted Lacie. That's a long story for another day. Mrs. Chantilly didn't have any children of her own. Least not that I heard about."

We moved onto discussion of back to school schedules. She'd be going back to her fulltime job teaching pre-K in only a few weeks. I understood all the hard work teachers go to before the school year starts.

"I'll be starting at Millicent the same week…" Yelling interrupted my train of thought and we both turned to the back corner of the deli.

"Stop pushing so hard. What does it matter, anyway? You got Caleb into rehab. What's the big deal?"

I wasn't sure, but I thought it was Shane Buchanan shouting. He stood up as if to leave, and the older man grabbed his arm.

"Don't you walk away from me. We aren't done yet. Not by a long shot."

Shane was pulled back down. "He's not my kid, remember. Can't Del keep track of his own son?"

I saw one of the other men take a swing at Shane, knocking him to the floor.

"My son was doing fine until he and Luke visited you around Derby time. Both of them started acting weird and it wasn't like they got the horse bug. That's why Brandon and I made the decision to put them in the camps this summer. To keep them busy and engaged in something besides trouble. What happened up there, Shane?"

Shane righted himself and his chair. "Don't blame me, Del. No proof of anything. Though Brandon, the way Luke went after the ladies, you might need to do some checking. That boy better buy stock in some condom company." He snickered and the other man stood up.

"Sit down. And stop making a scene. We aren't the only ones in here."

As they looked around, I turned away and shielded my face. I only hoped with my hair up, Shane wouldn't recognize me. It was early for lunch and there was only one other table with two women. One of them reminded me of the pushy neighborhood mom, Ashley something. Like us, they talked to themselves and hoped to be invisible.

Melina whispered, "Shall we leave? Or hang around and see what happens next?"

"We need Sally to bring us the check." I looked toward the kitchen and couldn't see anyone. "Maybe she's hiding. I wonder if they meet here and have family disagreements often."

A crash from the back and we turned to watch the fight between brothers, the chair now a couple feet from the skirmish. Blake and the third brother, Brandon, joined the fray. I wasn't sure if Brandon was going to help Del or what. Blake managed to somehow get between Del and

Shane, but not without taking a punch himself.

Del stepped back, hands up. Blake turned around. Shane was rubbing his jaw with one hand. I couldn't see the other hand.

"Shane, what's going on? I know Margie and you split. I talked to your sons last night and they told me. We're family and family sticks together. You know anything about the drugs my grandsons got involved with?"

"Family sticks together, right? Then where were you and my brothers when I had the State Police and the gaming commission come after me, breathing down my neck?"

"Son, sometimes help isn't obvious, but did you really think you got away with a few sanctions with your hostile attitude? You wanted to get in the horse racing business and I set you up. All you had to do was stay within the law and do it right. You got in trouble all by yourself just like you did when you were a teenager. I never should have let you get away with all the stuff you did, but your mom had your back."

"I never could live up to your expectations and be like Del and Brandon. It's only fitting it's their sons in trouble now." He laughed and it was all Blake could do to keep the brothers from going after Shane again.

Del hissed. "There's one problem with all this, Shane. You. Caleb already admitted to using and dealing to feed his habit. He'll be in rehab for a while. Thankfully, the doctors said his habit wasn't cocaine, though that's what he was dealing. It was some painkiller. Something he told them he took when he got thrown from a horse. Yeah, when he visited you. He told us he got thrown, had a concussion. Never mentioned opioids. Opioids he got from you."

"Shane, is that right, what Del said? You gave him opioids? Where'd you get them? Is that his source and who he's dealing for?" Blake's voice rose as he took a step toward his youngest.

Shane never got a chance to answer as Chief Peabody and two officers chose that moment to walk in. The chief nodded to us and the other table of ladies as he turned the "Open" sign to "Closed." He walked straight back, the two officers following him.

"I got a call there was a disturbance here." He looked around and then back to the men. "I think somebody owes Sally for the busted chair."

"Not a problem, Glenn. I'll take care of the chair and the checks for those ladies. We didn't mean to be disturbing anyone. We're all tense with what happened with Caleb and Luke and the drug money. A little unnerved is all."

"I appreciate you're tense. Interesting don't you think that some of the drug money ended up with Stories' body. And then there's the tale of how the boys' prints ended up on a certain yellow Highlander. There's no record they ever rented that car, even for long enough to drive it away and bring it back. And the rental company, they don't let people do test drives. Yet, their prints are in the car, Caleb's on the steering wheel, the mirror, the visor, the door handle. Luke's on the passenger side, same thing."

He let the information sink in and I couldn't stop watching this scene play out. Blake paled but recovered when Del moved to punch Shane again.

"Del, calm down. None of this is Shane's fault." He turned to Shane. "Right?"

Shane threw up his arms, an exaggerated shrug and didn't answer. He smirked as Blake shifted his attention back to the Chief

"Del, Brandon, I'll be talking with your sons again as soon as their attorneys are available. They're minors so you're invited as well. Blake, you need to settle up with Sally and then you all need to get out of here. She has a business to run."

On cue, Sally approached the group. Blake smiled at her, apologized and handed her some money. "Hopefully, that covers everything." To his sons, he ordered, "Get your stuff and let's go."

The chief cleared his throat. "Until this is resolved, please don't plan on any long trips – that applies to all of you, including you, Shane. If I hear you're on the road, I will put you in protective custody. We understand each other?"

Shane's face turned red and he took a step before Blake stopped him. "We understand. Shane'll be at my place. His mom wants to see him anyway."

Chief Peabody followed as the Buchanans exited. He stopped at the door. "Sally, can we inconvenience you for a few more minutes here?"

She looked at the money in her hand. "Take all the time you need. Ladies, you're all paid up. Need any refills?"

We all shook our heads and the other two ladies stood to go. "Sorry, but my officers need to get a statement from each of you."

One officer moved to the other table. The chief and the second officer came to our table.

"Jonas, can you take Ms. Melina's statement while I speak with... uh, Mrs. McMann and get her statement?"

There was an awkward minute when no one moved. The chief waved his arm, signaling me to move to a vacant table and I got the message. He asked me what happened and I told him.

"Caleb and Luke already confessed to planting the money, so Maddie and Alex are in the clear. I already shared the information on the Highlander with Brett. Funny thing, I got a call from Chief Hirsch." His eyes twinkled. "Any insights, Dr. Hendley of Cold Creek?"

I chuckled. "None you haven't already thought of given your comments to Shane. He's involved some how. If only in getting Caleb hooked on the opioids to begin with, maybe more."

He nodded and stood up. "You ladies are free to go. Someone turn the sign back to "Open" on your way out. I think we may have to give Sally some business and have our lunch here. Hopefully, nothing will interrupt our meal."

CHAPTER 23

My next stop was the grocery store. The interchange among the Buchanans kept coming to mind as I moved between the aisles. My gut told me Brett was right about Blake. He might be a lot of things, but nothing criminal. It also bothered me that one of them, probably Shane, had followed me.

At home, I was distracted when my contract and several other documents landed in my Inbox. The contract was standard legal verbiage and the salary for the year was higher than Dr. Addison indicated. I was happy with the terms. Unlike my previous contracts, this one included a paragraph stating very clearly this was for one year and one year only. So be it.

The rest of the packet included a list of the courses I'd be teaching in fall and spring, as well as syllabi. For all but one, I'd taught something similar and could adapt what I already had. Human Sexuality I'd never taught. Kim taught it though so I called her.

"How are you? Everything calmed down there? I caught a quick news alert about a drug bust."

"They identified two boys in the camp Maddie went to and now she and her friend Alex are in the clear. What a relief."

"What about Stories' murder? Was he connected to the drugs?"

"The murder investigation is still open. A drug deal gone wrong is one possibility. Or maybe he was trying to get the two boys to turn themselves in and one of them killed him. At least we think we know who tried to force me off the road. The same two boys. At least two of the mysteries may be solved."

"Did you get the contract for Millicent yet?"

"Yes, and that's why I'm calling. I have to teach Human Sexuality. Can you email me all your stuff?"

"Sure, and with all the time it'll save you, what are you going to do for fun?"

Laughing, I answered, "Want to come up here, maybe go to Lake Chesdin and go kayaking or hiking? There's only three more weeks before the semester starts."

"I'll see what Marty has on his calendar. Maybe come up next weekend? Would that work?"

"Probably. I'll check with Brett."

We chatted a little more about Cold Creek and Max.

***

Before I knew it, Maddie came home. Her bright smile told me she was having a good day.

"Everything go okay today?"

"Yes. Mr. Simpson apologized to Alex in front of the whole camp. He made sure everyone knew Alex was innocent. It was kind of awkward to be back after being gone for a week. A couple of kids asked where I'd been. I … I said I was doing stuff with family. Is that okay?"

"Well, you were so that's not an outright lie. Anybody say anything about Luke or Caleb?"

"MaryJane said Caleb was in the hospital from drugs. Nothing about Luke, though every time the door opened, I expected him to show up. Is he in jail?"

"I don't think so. Not in the hospital either."

Maddie sat down on the floor and Charlie crawled into her lap. "Can we take Charlie to see Bella again? When can Bella come home?"

I shrugged. "We'll see what your dad says when he gets home. In the meantime, I'll get dinner ready and you can set the table."

***

Instead of camp, the next day I took Maddie to the pet store and we picked up a crate and bed for Bella though I had a feeling Bella'd be spending time in Maddie's bed not her own. We also picked up a leash and dog toys. We got to Pets and Paws a little later than I usually arrive. Mrs. Chantilly and Melina were in the reception area when we walked in.

"Oh, good. Now I don't have to explain twice. Not that I should have to explain, mind you, but I will. Maybe then you can temper your reactions and not come stomping out to find me." She gave Melina a pointed look. Melina shrugged.

"Now, this is a trial. Blake Buchanan expects Luke will get probation and community service. That means they have to have some place willing to take Luke, and Caleb has about used up all the good neighbor feelings. Did you know, when I took over this house, there were almost a dozen strays? My grandmother and me, we take in strays and we make them people friendly. Seems to be nothing like having to clean up after a bunch of dogs to take that arrogance down a peg or two. Don't you agree?"

Melina gave her raised eyebrows and a grimace and I shook my head. "I'm lost here."

Mrs. Chantilly huffed. "Maddie, why don't you and Charlie go visit Brown Sugar and the pups."

Maddie didn't need any more encouragement and she disappeared. Only then did Mrs. Chantilly continue.

"The police are going to figure out it was Luke and Caleb who ran you off the road. Caleb may have been behind the steering wheel, but in reality Luke and his ego were driving the car and the whole mess with the money and Alex Champlin. Plain and simple. I need some help here with the dogs. More coming in I hear from the vet. I've moved more crates into the small dog area."

"Is Luke going to work here?"

Melina nodded. "With the big dogs in the back. Headphones in his ears and swearing."

I was speechless.

"Headphones will go. You two. You know those dogs back there and the routine. He needs to learn those routines and behave while he's doing them. If he gives anyone trouble or tries to charm the dogs to clean their own runs, well, I'll have a few words with him and his grandpa. You taking Bella home today, Sheridan? And what's this about you having a job? Congratulations."

She turned and walked toward the kitchen. Melina shook her head.

"She has no idea what she has agreed to. Dealing with Blake Buchanan has to be trouble."

Mrs. Chantilly came back around the corner. "I've been dealing with Blake since we were in school together. You know what they say about old people and memory loss? Not me, I remember all his shenanigans, not just his charming ways. I told him a long time ago Shane needed a firmer hand. Now, it's too late. Maybe not for Luke." Her voice softened at the end and she disappeared.

"I'll put my bag in a locker and join you back there. May be a great opportunity to teach him some manners."

When I walked into the big dog area, Mrs. Chantilly was pulling the earphones out with one hand and had her other hand out. Luke's face was getting redder by the minute, his hands clenched by his sides. Melina stepped closer.

"The phone, Luke. Now. Or do I call your grandpa?"

He hesitated and then pulled his phone out of pocket and placed it in her hand. "Back to work, now and you listen to these ladies. Do what they tell you to."

She turned around and walked away. The silence was too awkward for me. Chloe whimpered. I walked over to her cage and got her out.

"I'll take Chloe outside and maybe give her a bath. Is the shampoo out there, Melina?"

Luke turned and did a double take as Melina answered, "Yup, conditioner too if she needs it."

I took refuge outside despite the heat, and managed to get wet enough to cool off in the process of bathing Chloe. Melina came out with a dog I'd not seen before. Another at least part Shepard. I finished with Chloe and left her in the outside run and went back inside. Her crate was cleaned out and a clean blanket and fresh water waiting for her.

I looked for the roster where we noted who's gotten taken care of last. Luke handed it to me.

"Thank you. It looks like Barley needs to get some exercise and his crate cleaned. Where is Barley?" I handed him back the clipboard and looked around. Truly a mix of mixes, the color of Barley, I attached a leash to the dog and led him to join Melina.

"I'm not thinking this is going to work, having Luke here. He's sullen and angry. What do you think?"

Shrugging my shoulders, I answered in a whisper. "He is now, but he may figure out how to charm the dogs and Mrs. Chantilly. He's lucky anyone is willing to give him a chance right now. I sure wouldn't."

"I guess. That's how she ended up adopting Lacie. Dogs aren't the only strays she takes in."

I shrugged again and got to work. On the plus side, we managed to get more dogs bathed with Luke cleaning out the crates. When I went to check on Maddie and Charlie, I saw Luke over with the Dane mix, Danish. He spoke softly as he rubbed the girl's belly.

"Sheridan? Are we ready to go home? Mrs. Chantilly says Bella can come home, too."

Rather than have her upset by seeing Luke, I turned her around and out of the room as I yelled, "See ya, Melina. I'll call you later."

We collected Charlie, Bella, and the gift basket from Mrs. Chantilly. Together with our goodies from the pet store, we were all set for the new addition. Or might have been if Bella didn't get sick in the car.

CHAPTER 24

I was taken a little off guard when Brett came home with someone pulling in behind him. Obviously, someone Brett knew as he leaned against his car waiting for the man to join him. They were laughing as they walked in.

"Sheridan, this is James Zabry, the detective who most often covers any local issues."

"Hi James, nice to meet you. Can I get you some coffee? Water?"

"Nice to meet you, too, Sheridan. Water will be fine."

I grabbed a bottle of water for him and waited.

"James is now investigating the drug dealing of Luke and Caleb. They definitely took it outside the county and still may have something to do with why

Stories was killed and by whom."

"Great. The sooner this is solved the better."

"I'm going to let James fill you in on the afternoon updates."

"The police up by Lynchburg confirmed Luke and Caleb were carded at a local nightclub and there was a report from security they tried to crash some party. A couple other run-ins but no charges were filed. For high school kids, it struck the police as odd they'd keep popping up. At the area colleges and at the high schools. Nothing confirmed yet, but not inconsistent with dealing."

"With them familiar with Lynchburg, it would be easy for them to figure out your route and hide before coming at you in the Highlander. If they were dealing drugs up there, they probably have places to hide. It's looking more and more like it was them in the Highlander, Sher."

"Uh, I have the update, Brett," James interrupted. "It's confirmed. Caleb admits to stealing the car and driving the car, with instructions to cause you to have an accident. He said he did it with Luke's help. Muttered something about his uncle, but didn't specify which one. His lawyer kept trying to shut him up. When I asked him which uncle, he denied saying anything at all."

"What did Luke say? Why try to run us off the road?" It made no sense to me.

James continued, "Luke isn't talking. His attorney is much happier than Caleb's. The other interesting thing? Blake Buchanan isn't talking either. Nobody, including Caleb is talking about the murder."

"Caleb was the one who called it in. Luke was there with him when the police arrived. Did one of them kill him? Or do they know or suspect who killed him?" Brett voiced the questions we'd contemplated.

"Those are the questions Chief Peabody is trying to answer. Me? I'm most interested in where Caleb was getting his opioids and the cocaine. Peabody suggested we start with a check on Shane's gambling and horse racing at the same time. Not sure if he suspects something or what. Any ideas, Brett? You pulled that case last time."

Brett shrugged. "No idea. I haven't heard anything about it since the problems were resolved. I did think it was odd Blake had Shane come down. Maybe Blake knows more than he's letting on."

"The gambling thing did come up in their fighting today. After witnessing his behavior today, I wouldn't trust Shane." I shook my head. "The brothers weren't too happy with his responses either."

"That's what Peabody said. I'm going to get going. I have a meeting with him in about an hour. Hopefully, he got more out of Caleb or Luke or Blake. Heck, maybe someone confessed." He laughed and Brett walked him out.

We got dinner on the table and I called for Maddie. She hesitated at the door, Bella in her arms, Charlie at her feet.

"What's wrong?"

"I fell asleep and ... and Bella had an accident." She looked about ready to cry.

Brett chuckled. "She's a puppy and you have to train her. For now, put her in her crate and wash your hands. After dinner, we'll start crate and house training."

With Bella in the crate, Charlie took her place next to the crate as if to keep Bella company.

***

After dinner, I cleaned up and let Brett explain how to crate and house train Bella. It was still early and not too hot. I was feeling a bit restless.

"How about we take both dogs for a walk to the neighborhood park? Bella might get tired and you might have to carry her some, though."

"Yes, let's do that!"

Brett agreed and we leashed both dogs. I was pretty sure Bella'd never been on a leash. She kept trying to catch it. We hadn't gotten very far and Bella lay down. For now, she wasn't heavy and Maddie picked her up.

Brett patted his pocket. "Hold up. I forgot my phone. Must have laid it down somewhere."

"Bella isn't exactly walking. We could all go back."

"No, I want to take Bella to the park and Charlie needs her walk." Maddie pouted.

"I'll go back and get it and meet you at the park, okay?"

"Sure."

He turned and set off for home. In the meantime, Maddie and I arrived at the park. I heard someone and stopped. I recognized Mrs. Chantilly's voice.

"Shane Miles Buchanan, you shame your family. Your father is beside himself, never mind your mother."

"You asked me to meet you here to yell at me? You don't know anything, old woman." He chortled.

Realizing it was Shane, I took both leashes and whispered, "Maddie, run back and tell your dad to hurry, okay? Be quiet." She nodded, put Bella down, and took off. I edged forward so I could see them and hoped neither dog barked.

"No respect. That's why I prefer dogs most times to people. You got yourself hooked on opioids, didn't you?"

"So what? I was in pain and my doctor prescribed them. They made me feel good even when I didn't need them any more. Easy enough to get doctors to prescribe them."

"And then you started dealing drugs? To pay for your habit. Or were you already dealing?"

"You don't get it. Used to be I could make money selling pot. Once they legalized it even for medical, that avenue wasn't going to last. I needed money and dealing coke was profitable."

"You mean you gambled too heavily and lost. You owed someone money and they offered you a way out. Your banking tells a story as good as any."

"How'd you…? Doesn't matter. Nothing matters. This will all blow over, you'll see."

"Did Stories not mind his own business? Is that why you killed him?"

"He was one of those liberals. Help the poor.

163

Help the disabled. Help the addicts. Stories wasn't a Buchanan and he had it in for me. He got on Caleb's case. Somehow figured out the boy was hooked. He threatened to tell my father, get him involved. Not happening. I set up the meeting with him. Stories thought I was going to agree with him – the two of us would get Luke and Caleb out of this mess." He snorted.

"I guess he was surprised to find out you were the one who got him hooked and kept him supplied. Your father's figured it out already. And by extension that you were some how involved in their dealing. He's still trying not to acknowledge you're the person responsible for Stories death. It's going to kill him when he finds out."

He shrugged. "Manipulating my father is my favorite past time. I've about got him convinced Stories was the distributor and it must have been a drug deal gone bad. He certainly had easier access to those two than I do. I live an hour away from here in a different county. So I gave Caleb opioids when he was thrown from a horse. How was I supposed to know he'd get hooked and turn to illegal means to support his habit? Take my word for it, those two won't say nothing, and they weren't there when I killed him."

"But they think you killed him?"

"Heck, no. I ducked into the tree line when I heard someone coming. Caleb ran into the trees and puked. Luke too. Once Caleb called the cops, I hightailed it out of there. They'd told me about the kids they set up. I took advantage of their mess with that other kid and dumped the gun. Then called in the anonymous tip. They're psyched it looks like Stories was into drugs, too."

Mrs. Chantilly threw up her arms and shook her head. "You don't even care about the fall out. If this old woman figured it out, don't you think those detectives will?"

With a maniacal laugh, he commented, "It was icing on the cake, his daughter was part of their set up. But seriously, you really shouldn't be confronting people. Not very smart. Not too many people here tonight – too hot." He pulled out a gun. I instinctively backed up and gasped as I collided with Brett as Charlie barked his greeting. Zabry was there, too.

"Did you hear that, Shane. Someone else is here. How many people you going to kill?"

Much to my dismay, after a slight pause Brett stepped out in the open, his gun drawn. "Let her go, Shane. You're drugged up and probably can't shoot straight."

I watched as Shane looked from Mrs. Chantilly to Brett. He snorted again. "It'll be my pleasure to kill you first, Detective." He laughed again.

I heard a shot and screamed. Shane was holding his arm and Brett was still standing. Nobody dead. Zabry emerged from the trees. He handed Brett his weapon and cuffed Shane. Brett picked up Shane's gun.

I tried to join them and had to pick up Bella. She was curled up fast asleep. Mrs. Chantilly sat down on a bench. Tears streamed down her face and Brett gave her his handkerchief. Zabry called Peabody and we waited.

CHAPTER 25

The weekend came soon enough and with it, a visit from Kim and Marty. We decided to postpone the trip to Lake Chesdin until Bella was trained and able to travel with us. Instead we hosted an end of summer and "murder solved" celebration. The news hadn't broadcast a lot of details. Blake Buchanan had the social capital to limit what went public. I'd only shared the ending with Kim over the phone.

We were able to reserve some tables and a grill at one of the town parks south of us. A short drive and the park had plenty of trees as well as swings, a volleyball court, horseshoes, and bocce ball. Maddie was the sentry with Charlie and Bella to direct others as they arrived.

With everyone carrying something, chips and dip,

garden salad, fruit salad, and cole slaw were set up along with condiments, rolls, paper plates and plastic forks. Brett and Marty got the grill going with hamburgers and hot dogs. Eric Pinsky joined us much to Marty's delight. After introductions, Eric didn't waste any time.

"Before everyone gets here, can someone fill me in on the rest of the story?" Once Alex and Maddie were cleared, he hadn't been in the loop on the rest of the situations.

Kim chimed in with "Us too. I only got the tail end," and Marty nodded. I tipped my head to Brett.

"Luke and Caleb set Alex and Maddie up for theft – and inadvertently for drugs. That's where this all started. They stole the pizza money and then called in the anonymous tip. They also called in the accusations against Angie and the tip Alex's father had murdered Stories. Some of that may have been helped along by Shane, but we'll never prove it. It was Shane who left a box with 'goodies' in it for Maddie."

I shuddered. "What about taking Karla's walker?"

"Nothing to do with any of this. A new orderly thought it didn't belong there and put it in their equipment closet."

With everyone's nods, he continued. "It was Shane, with Caleb in the car, who tried to force us into a ditch. When the boys spotted Maddie in Lynchburg, they called Shane. He was afraid somehow Sheridan and Maddie being there had something to do with the drug set up and told them to steal a car and run them off the road. By then both boys were in too deep to Shane so they followed his directions."

I interjected, "Shane's problem was that while Caleb was an addict and that made him an easy target, it also made him the weak link. He admitted to driving the Highlander and to being addicted."

"So how did Stories fit in, aside from being a Civil War buff?"

"Nothing to do with the Civil War, Marty. At some point in his business training, he worked with a drug rehab group and spent time with addicts. That's why he was so vocal about their needs and rehabilitation. On the few family occasions he interacted with Caleb, he suspected he was addicted. He'd also heard rumors about Luke's behavior and both boys dealing drugs, probably from his sons. At some point, he managed to talk to Caleb and tried to get him to rehab. Caleb told Shane he'd threatened to tell his grandfather, Blake. That put a target on Stories' back."

"Didn't Shane realize it was all a house of cards?"

"You'd think so, wouldn't you? Keep in mind, Eric, that Shane was on opioids and who knows what else. He had huge gambling debts and couldn't refuse when the people he owed money told him to do something. His wife suspected the drug problem and the gambling. She told him to get help or get out. He told her to leave if she couldn't live with him. To his surprise, she did. When Blake called her, she told Blake about the erratic deposits and withdrawals in their bank account. She'd also discovered he had a

169

bank account he had money hidden in. The feds are looking into all of that in case he was laundering money."

"I still don't understand how Mrs. Chantilly knew about all of that and other stuff." I shook my head.

"You told me she mentioned growing up with Blake. Zabry said he looked into her background at some point with the same questions you have. She grew up here and the high school yearbook at least has her and Blake an item. Her mother and she moved away after she graduated and Blake went to college and got married. When her grandmother died and left her the house and dogs, she moved back. Even in high school, they were not in the same social class and by the time she returned, he was married and the mayor. She became a recluse, having more contact with the stray dogs and the volunteers who helped out than anyone else."

"So how did she get her information? Neither Melina nor I were giving her these details."

Brett smiled. "Obviously, since the woman is rarely seen outside of the house, no one can say for sure, but it seems she and Blake still talk frequently. From what his wife told Zabry, Blake consulted with her on town issues when he was mayor. They only disagreed when it came to how he raised his sons, especially Shane."

"Is there a Mr. Chantilly some place? Melina didn't think she had any children of her own."

"Chantilly is her maiden name. The 'Mrs'? Her choice, I guess. The other tidbit Zabry found would resonate with you, Eric. She routinely would take in youth who got in trouble with the law. One every few years. Lacie was her most recent before Luke."

Shouts and whistles interrupted the post mortem on Stories' murder. Angie, Alex, and Karla arrived, along with Duke. Nedra, Melina, and Vincent arrived at about the same time. Introductions over, the males took over the grill and the kids headed for activities. Duke accompanied Karla, while Charlie and Bella hung out with us. We discussed my new job, even if it was temporary. I was sure something would come up in the next year.

Eric chimed in, "It sounded like Chief Peabody also may be calling on you for assistance, if not the State Police. That might keep you out of trouble."

Brett snorted. "More likely it will keep her in trouble. I'm hoping the teaching position at the college will keep her busy."

Marty gravitated to Eric, no doubt to talk law, politics, and their shared acquaintances. I overheard mention of the Civil War reenactment at the historical park. Kim, Angie, Melina, and I played with the dogs.

As everyone ate and chatted, I looked around and decided I was going to like this new place. One thing for sure, I was never going to complain about being bored again.

Author's notes

I hoped you liked the first in the Sheridan Hendley series. Although it is a spinoff of the Cold Creek series, each book can be read as a stand alone. New fan of Sheridan? You may want to check out the Cold Creek series if you haven't read it to see how she ended up with Brett and Maddie.

About Christa Nardi
Christa Nardi is an avid reader with her love of mysteries beginning with Nancy Drew and other teen mysteries. Her favorite authors have shifted from Carolyn Keene and Earl Stanley Gardner to more contemporary mystery and crime authors over time. Christa has been a long time writer from poetry and short stories to mystery series.

You can find Christa Nardi at:
- Amazon author page
  http://www.amazon.com/-/e/B00G8SBCKK
- Facebook:
  https://www.facebook.com/christa.nardi.5
- Twitter: https://twitter.com/ChristaN7777
- Email: cccnardi@gmail.com
- Sign up for the monthly newsletter with updates and sale/new release announcements
  http://smarturl.it/NardiNewsletter